MARINA'S SISTER

'*You ought to stop feeling sorry for yourself!*'—that's paediatrician Simon Harraday's advice to Nurse Vicky Jardine. But how can she, when all her life she's lived in her beautiful sister Marina's shadow? Goaded by Dr Harraday's taunts, Vicky accepts a job in his London clinic and begins to find happiness in their work together. Until, that is, she discovers his relationship with Marina . . .

Books you will enjoy
in our Doctor Nurse series

MARINA'S SISTER

BY

BARBARA PERKINS

MILLS & BOON LIMITED
London · Sydney · Toronto

Copyright © Barbara Perkins 1983
First published as a serial in Great Britain 1983 by
Woman's Weekly

This edition published 1984 by
Mills & Boon Limited, 15–16 Brook's Mews
London W1A 1DR

Australian copyright 1984
Philippine copyright 1984

ISBN 0 263 74724 7

Set in 10 on 11 pt Linotron Times
03–0684–57,990

Photoset by Rowland Phototypesetting Ltd
Bury St Edmunds, Suffolk
Made and printed in Great Britain by
Richard Clay (The Chaucer Press) Ltd
Bungay, Suffolk

CHAPTER ONE

'*YOUR presence is requested at the marriage of Marina Elizabeth, elder daughter of Dr and Mrs P. F. Jardine, and Andrew John Morton of Morton's Farm, Pensbury Village . . .*'

Vicky knew the invitation off by heart, and the words seemed to echo through her head all the way through the ceremony as she stood alone behind Marina as her bridesmaid. It was better than having to listen to her lovely, clever sister repeating her vows, and Andrew repeating his. She knew that it was mean-spirited of her not to want to listen, just as she knew she ought not to be asking herself why Marina ever had to come home. After all, Andrew had never treated Vicky as anything other than a friend—the local doctor's second daughter who had trained as a nurse at the hospital in the nearby new town, and whose home was the next house to the farm. He had taken her out occasionally, and let her come over and help at the farm at harvest-time. But then he hadn't shown any particular interest in any of the other girls in the district until Marina came home for a rare weekend from her job as a doctor in a London hospital.

Beautiful, bright Marina. Tall, slender and striking where Vicky was small and ordinary, laughing and vivacious where Vicky was capable but quiet. Vicky had never really minded being overshadowed by her prettier, more accomplished sister because she had always loved and admired her—and besides, with four years between them Vicky had been too young to feel the competition before Marina left home to go to medical school at a top teaching hospital. She had seen her popularity all through their growing up, and her skill at attracting the boys without any apparent effort, but it had been easy to admire her for it, and to bask just a little in the reflected glory of being Marina Jardine's sister. Now, having to play her part in Marina's wedding and try to look happy for her—to *be* happy for her—it was less easy.

They came out of church, posed for photographs, then walked in a happy laughing procession through the village to the doctor's house on the far edge of it, where a striped marquee was set up in the garden ready for the reception and caterers had been working since early morning. Vicky helped to show everyone where to go, smiled sweetly at all the uncles and aunts and cousins, and tried to keep out of the way of Marina's London friends who had the sort of sophistication which made her feel plain and inadequate. Fortunately, once everyone was in the marquee enjoying the buffet laid out on long tables, and chattering and gossiping and congratulating, it wasn't too difficult to avoid talking to anybody, simply by keeping moving. That was all she had to do—smile and move about and wait for it all to be over.

Luckily, there was no one who might guess her feelings, and she could tell herself wryly that nursing gave good practice in hiding her emotions. Her parents had had no idea of their younger daughter's feelings for the young farmer who had inherited his great-uncle's farm two years ago and came to join the village community. Certainly, Marina had no idea that when she came home and Andrew Morton's eyes lit up at the sight of her, her young sister's heart had felt a chill shock, like the withering of a frost-caught bud . . .

The speeches were over at last. Even the uncle who insisted on joking that 'Andrew did the traditional thing and married the girl next door!' had finally finished. Vicky, wincing involuntarily, covered it with a dutiful laugh—and suddenly found herself looking straight into the eyes of a wedding guest over on the far side of the marquee. He was one of Marina's London crowd, at least she supposed so because she had seen him with them, and his gaze was intent enough to make her flush and turn away, pretending to fiddle with the empty champagne glass she had just put down. He looked like someone who would be a friend of Marina's anyway. They all seemed to be tall and smooth and successful-looking, with the same careless elegance and patina of confidence. This one was somehow even more so than most—tall enough to see over most people's heads, darkly noticeable, and with an aristocratic nose to look down, like a Jane Austen hero. He was far more Marina's type than Andrew was . . . Oh, it wasn't fair! As this childish thought rose unbidden from her heart, Vicky felt the prick of tears in her throat. They were tears she had been firmly controlling for weeks, and she certainly couldn't let them fall now. Swallowing quickly and presenting a blank, smiling face, she edged through the crowd and slipped out of the open tent entrance. No one would miss her for half an hour if she slipped away to her favourite refuge in the small, neglected orchard at the end of the garden, well out of the way of all the wedding guests because the shrubbery grew between.

It was quiet in the orchard. The festive hum retreated into the background and she could stand still and be aware of country noises. A light breeze rustled the tops of the trees, sending dancing patterns of sunlight across the rough grass. A woodpigeon called out sleepily in the summer air and somewhere a lark was rising and singing in a high, sweet ripple. Vicky leaned her hands against the rough weathered wood of the top bar of the fence and gazed out across the fields unseeingly, resting her eyes blindly on the bright yellow of a field of rape with its colour intensified by the sun. If only she was unselfish enough, she thought desolately, she should be glad that Andrew's fair, square-featured face had looked so happy. It would be easier if she could have plunged straight back into the consolation of work, but she was just at the start of four weeks' holiday, and she could hardly ask to change them when everyone had said how lucky it was that she could start her holiday with her sister's wedding. So she had all these empty weeks to fill—and she would have to look carefree in them so that her parents didn't notice anything. And everyone would want to talk about the wedding endlessly. And then Marina and Andrew would be coming back from their honeymoon and settling into the farm which Vicky cycled past every day to get to the station and catch the train which took her to work. She would see them together and she would have to go *on* looking carefree, and cheerful, and *sisterly* . . .

'You ought to stop feeling sorry for yourself!'

The deep voice behind her made her jump round. Six feet away, incongruously elegant amongst the untended trees and so tall that a small branch was brushing the dark hair away from his forehead, stood the man who had caught her eye in the marquee.

'Wh-what—?'

'—am I doing here? I followed you.' He put up a languid hand to push the branch out of the way and strolled to join her at the fence, casting a swift, uninterested glance at the fields and hedges spread out in the sunlight. 'An undistinguished view, but scarcely worth crying over. Neither is the bridegroom worth crying over. After all, he *has* just married someone else, hasn't he?'

He could have sounded kind, but he didn't, he sounded mocking. Vicky stiffened and put a hasty hand up to her cheek. Yes, there *were* tears there. She made to rub them away, then remembered that her hands would be greeny from the fence. She tried for a wobbly laugh, which came out more like a gulp, and said swiftly, 'I don't know what you're talking about! It's traditional to cry at weddings!'

'Don't be so prim and proper. I watched you carefully avoiding watching him right through the ceremony. You were stuck out in the middle of the aisle, after all, and one has to look at something.' He inspected the fence with apparent distaste, then leaned an elbow on it, which brought his towering height nearer to her level. From a distance they would have looked like a friendly couple having a pleasant conversation, Vicky thought crossly, but his dark hazel eyes were fixed on her with that mocking gleam in them—and he was still looking down his aristocratic nose. This time, at her. 'Don't worry, I don't suppose anyone else noticed. Most people watch the bride at weddings. I didn't particularly want to look at her, so I looked at you instead. I suppose he was your boyfriend before he was Marina's, is that it? Well, if you fought for him and lost, he isn't worth having, is he? But you must like being a sacrificial lamb, or you wouldn't go and be bridesmaid as well!'

Vicky had been tempted to point out bitterly that one didn't, *couldn't*, fight the Marinas of this world—but he looked far too much the type who had never been second best to anyone to understand that. Besides, his last words brought her mouth closed with an angry snap. She swallowed, then said with as much dignity as she could muster, 'I think you've got it all wrong, Mr—er—'

'Simon Harraday. And doctor, not mister.' He was looking at her with one eyebrow raised, as if he expected her to recognise the name. When she didn't, he gave a moody shrug. 'I trained at the same hospital as Marina, though I was a couple of years ahead of her. And no, I'm not wrong about you. I rarely am, and besides, I'm observant. It's all the clinical training, you know.' His mouth had a sarcastic twist. 'I observed that you found the wedding as depressing as I did, and it didn't take long to realise why. What on earth has the man got to fascinate both of you? He didn't look much of a catch to me. Or is it just that rustic charm and gumboots are in this season?'

His dry sarcasm was unbearable. So was the attack on Andrew. Vicky burst out, 'Andrew is kind, and—and sincere, and he's very—very—'

'He'll have to be *very* all sorts of things to keep Marina amused out here in the depths of the country,' Simon commented, filling in the pause where she had broken off with the realisation that she was betraying herself. He went on, 'She's supposed to be mad about medicine, and suddenly she's throwing it all up to be a farmer's wife! Didn't your father have anything to say about it? You seem to be a thoroughly medical family, after all. Oh yes, I know about you, even if you've never heard of me. You're little sister Vicky who's training to be a nurse.'

'Trained, as it happens. I'm a staff nurse, not a student!'

'Really? That just shows how long it is since she told me. I remember you stayed to train locally, but looking at you, I thought you were about eighteen. My apologies, Staff Nurse.' He made her a mocking half-bow from his leaning position close beside her, looming over her in a way which made her feel faintly overwhelmed. He was still studying her, and that made her feel overwhelmed too. He was the kind of man Vicky normally saw at a distance, or in photographs of the rich and famous. Even his voice was right for one of the beautiful people; deep, velvety, slightly drawling. And challenging. As if today hadn't been bad enough already, he was making her feel confused, stupid and inadequate.

She stared back at him with dislike and found herself saying tartly, 'If you're so worried about Marina giving up medicine, I expect Daddy will give her a partnership in the practice if she wants one! He was saying that he could do with another partner. And besides—'

'It's hospital medicine she's good at. She'd make a

hopeless GP. If you were going to say that it isn't my business, it is, because I hate seeing somebody wasted!'

'Dr Simon Harraday's one-man crusade against waste? Oh!' Vicky looked at him with her eyes suddenly wide. Was that it, then? The reason why he didn't particularly want to look at Marina during the wedding? Because he was waiting for her to go on, with one eyebrow raised interrogatively, she blurted out, 'You must be the Simon who . . . I overheard one of Marina's friends saying it was surprising *Simon* had come to the wedding! Was she your—?'

'Suffice it to say that if I can get over Marina's defection, you can get over Andrew's. Anyway, we've talked enough about Marina. Though I must say,' he added, studying her, 'if it was her choice to dress you in that colour I'm surprised, because whatever else she is, she isn't normally spiteful. Girls with green eyes and brown hair should never wear that colour blue.'

Vicky had chosen the dress herself—after all, her much paler blue staff nurse's uniform suited her well enough—and she flushed. Simon Harraday's sarcastic gaze took it in, but he didn't make any kind of apology. Instead he let out an exasperated groan. 'No, *don't* for goodness' sake start crying again! Don't be so spineless—you'd try the patience of a plaster saint!'

'I am not crying! I just think you're appallingly rude and—and—'

'And why did I follow you anyway? Fellow-feeling? Someone to take it out on?' He glowered at her fiercely enough to make that last statement true. 'Maybe I was just bored with the whole ballyhoo in there, and wanted to look at some scenery instead! What sort of staff nurse are you, anyway?'

The suddenness of the question threw her, and her impulse to feel sorry for him had certainly died. It wasn't her fault if he was in love with Marina. And why, Vicky thought bitterly, did everyone have to be in love with Marina? 'What—sort?' she asked, puzzled.

'Yes. What speciality? Or did you just go where you were sent?'

'Oh, no. Children. I chose it.'

'Because you wanted to?'

'Yes, of course because I wanted to! People don't work on Kids unless they like children!'

'Oh yes they do, quite often. It might just have been your best chance of promotion, or the only job going which would keep you in the area. Hm, that could be remarkably convenient. Are you good at it?'

'Yes—I think so. Why?'

'Because you could get another job, couldn't you? One that would take you away from here? Or,' he asked savagely, 'had you planned on sticking around gazing devotedly at your farmer from a distance, like a poor relation in a Russian novel? Or not even from a distance! You could darn his socks when Marina didn't want to, couldn't you? While turning yourself into the archetypal lovesick maiden aunt, so that everyone has to feel guilty about poor little Victoria!'

'How *dare*—' Vicky was beginning, but he was already going on.

'Or of course there's Plan B, isn't there. Waiting until Marina's tired of country life and does a flit, so that you can step into the breach and heal the poor man's aching heart with your tender ministrations? I should warn you,' he added, rising abruptly to his full height and towering over her so that she had to glare up at him, 'if you're thinking of being as Victorian as your name and slapping my face, I shall simply pick you up bodily and throw you over the fence into the field!'

He looked as if he meant it. Vicky's hand, half-raised, dropped hastily to her side. She was alight with fury— but the nearest bit of the field was full of nettles. 'Go away!' she told him in a shaking voice.

'No chance. I'm going to offer you a job. Well, someone's got to protect Marina from having you under her feet while she's trying to settle down, haven't they?'

'You're—you're trying to protect Marina from *me*? She's my sister!'

'So she is, but stranger things have happened. Even murder's most likely to happen amongst close relations,' Simon said urbanely, 'and that's statistics, not guess-work! Not that I thought you were going to go all Gothic and poison her soup.' He was looking, suddenly, vastly amused, and in spite of her fury with him, Vicky couldn't help noticing that it made him look very attractive. Charming, handsome, and darkly devilish. His lips twitched in a laugh, and he said, 'You're very striking when you're angry, did you know? In the best sense, of course!'

Throwing her a casual compliment on top of all the rest was almost the last straw. Vicky lost the last rem-nants of her usual good manners. 'I'm not surprised Marina threw *you* over,' she told him acidly, 'it's prob-ably the most sensible thing she's done in years!'

'That's a nice healthy viewpoint. What about you, though? You're not really going to sit here being unfair competition, are you? And asking for sympathy?'

'I could never be unfair competition for Marina, and you know it, so there's no need to be so—to be even nastier! And I don't recall,' Vicky said, tilting her chin at a dangerously militant angle, 'ever asking for your sympathy, and I certainly haven't asked for anyone else's!'

'Good, then you can come back to London and work for me. When would you be able to get away? I really need someone now, but I suppose you'll have to give some notice? How long? Two weeks? Three?'

'Carefully clearing the end of the honeymoon?' Now that she had got the bit between her teeth, she could put almost as much sarcasm into her voice as he could. 'I have to give a month's notice, but as I'm just starting a four-week holiday, I could go now if I wanted to. But I can't imagine what sort of job you could offer me, and I can't imagine wanting to work for someone so—so dangerous!'

That made him burst out laughing, which wasn't the reaction she wanted at all. Laughter made him look vividly alive, the dark eyes sparkling, the mobile mouth losing its moody, sardonic twist. He really was unfairly attractive by anyone's reckoning when he laughed like that, so tall that Vicky only came up to his shoulder and lithe and slim as an athlete, wearing his clothes with an air which suggested he could look good in anything. He was also the most eminently dislikeable man Vicky had ever met, and she hastily reminded herself of the fact. Also, he was in love with Marina—of course. And if it wasn't her, it would be somebody like her. What devil had prompted him to come and torment Marina's plain little shadow of a sister was beyond imagining, but perhaps he simply had a taste for revenge against the whole family. She tilted her chin at him again, waiting for him to stop laughing. And go away. But he didn't, he just said,

'Dangerous is nice. I'm serious about the job, though. I am—though I'm sure you won't believe it—a paediatrician. I run a small clinic, which was left to me by my father. We happen to be short of nurses, permanent staff that is, and although agency nurses fill the gaps, they're not entirely satisfactory because there aren't many who have particular experience with children. You have the experience and you could do with a job. It couldn't fit better, could it? I might have asked you to give it a try even if you hadn't worked on a children's ward, but as you have, it's ideal!'

Ideal it might have been, if the offer had come from anyone else. Vicky felt a flicker of interest as he talked. But she couldn't imagine wanting to work for Simon

Harraday any more than she could actually imagine him being a children's specialist. Especially, she wouldn't want to work for Simon Harraday with the consciousness that he knew how she felt about her brother-in-law. On the other hand, *she* knew how *he* felt about Marina, didn't she? Angry and bitter, but also oddly protective, so he must have loved her rather a lot. Vicky felt her spirits sinking again and tried to stop them. It would be a marvellous way to get away from home, particularly when he wanted someone straight away and she had just been wondering what on earth she was going to do with her life. She looked dubiously at Simon Harraday, who seemed to be waiting for her answer, unless he was just watching her in that relaxed way because he was perfectly certain she would say yes because it would suit him if she did!

'*You* run a children's hospital?'

'I do. I may be appalling company, as I'm sure you were about to say, but I'm also a good doctor.'

'Did Marina—?'

'No, she didn't work with me, and why can't you forget about Marina? This is you we're talking about!'

'I suppose it's private medicine,' Vicky said. Knowing how the system worked, she thought she could recognise the signs and she wrinkled her nose a little at the thought of a private clinic, treating only rich children. 'I've been working in a new town hospital, and I'm not sure that I want to.'

'Illness isn't actually a privilege of the poor,' Simon said, giving her one of his sarcastic looks, 'and I do get a little tired of the attitude which doesn't take into account that some rich kids can be as neglected—even if in a different way—as poor ones! Yes, we do have some private patients, as it happens, but before you jump to any more instant conclusions, we're properly registered and totally above-board and more than half our patients come from the National Health! I might add, too, that the paying patients and the National Health ones get exactly the same facilities and treatment. What on earth do you think I'm doing—babysitting? Unnecessary cosmetic surgery on wealthy teenagers? I wouldn't touch it with a bargepole. No, and not under-age abortions either, though I've been asked!'

'I suppose you expect me to apologise . . .' Vicky began stiffly.

'No. It's a viewpoint I'm used to. I had enough of it when—but never mind that. All right, since it's fair that you might want to know a few details, I'll explain.' He gave her a moody look from under his eyebrows, but went on, with a touch of impatience. 'I had the chance to take over a rather run-down private clinic. For reasons of red tape, the Area Health Authority couldn't take it over and run it as a children's hospital, but as a private citizen, *I* could. As long as I keep around one third of the beds private I can run the place as I like, and take in National Health patients when I like. It seemed to me to be a good way of cutting down the waiting lists, whether it seems that way to you or not!'

'Yes, I see,' Vicky said, hastily revising her opinion. She looked at him thoughtfully. Since he had that glossy, successful look, she'd assessed him as very much the fashionable private doctor, so that the next question came out almost involuntarily. 'You yourself, are you solely in private practice?'

'As it happens, no! I'm Paediatric Consultant at a North London Hospital—as well as running the clinic. Any more questions?'

'What kind of cases do you have in the clinic?' Vicky asked quickly, ignoring the dry sarcasm in the last bit.

'The usual variety. Some are my own patients, some referred by other people. We're not geared to major or long-term therapy and if something would be better treated in a large hospital with all its facilities, I'll say so.

We do have a dialysis machine, bought out of the profits from the private side, which is in current regular use by one of my NHS patients. What else have we currently got? A couple of complex fractures, one a re-set. An appendix, a tonsils. A simple squint correction. All done by visiting surgeons. I'm on the medical side myself. We've got a chorea on bed-rest. Two children in for observation and tests, one of them a hyperactive who may respond to diet. An old-fashioned croup and a pneumonia. A mixed sample, as you can see.' He had been counting them off on his fingers. 'Oh, and there's also an unhappy little rubella, in isolation, but before you pour scorn on me, it's not my fault that his mother's pregnant and hasn't had her injections. I agreed to take him in as a private patient because there was literally nowhere else for him to go! So now, go ahead, and tell me *that* offends your socialist principles!'

'No,' Vicky said hastily. She liked him better when he was talking about work, because he was so plainly passionately interested in it and the interest lit his face with a lively intelligence. Though it was confusing to have to revise her opinion of him, she found she was interested in the job he was offering, half against her will. 'How many beds has the clinic got?' she asked.

'Twenty. Quite small, as you can see. Usually busy. One-to-one specialling for the most part, so you can see we need plenty of nurses. Well?' Simon said challengingly. 'Are you going to admit that sick children are sick children anywhere, and worth nursing anywhere? Come back to London with me and I'll give you plenty of employment. Since it's set up as I've explained, you'd get private sector pay, too, if that interests you!'

'Not outstandingly,' Vicky said drily, though more not to let him score a point than anything else. It didn't, however, seem to be the moment to get into a general discussion on nurses' pay and she was perfectly well aware that he was quite capable of pointing out that living at home must have made it easier for her to live on her pay. She was jerked back into realising that she was at home *now*, and in the middle of Marina's wedding which she had almost forgotten about in listening to him. They ought to go back to the wedding before too long. She swallowed hard, and said, 'Yes, all right, the job sounds interesting. But we haven't got over the main point, have we? Which,' she cast him a darkling look, 'is why on earth I would want to work for *you*!'

'Because I'm a doctor and you're a nurse. No better reason than that. You don't have to like me, all I'm asking you to do is work! And a very good solace for the heart it is,' he added—which was so much what she'd been thinking earlier that she might have felt some sympathy between them if he hadn't sounded so mocking again. 'You could change out of that dreadful dress, throw some clothes in a suitcase and drive back with me tonight. Unless of course you actually want to count the wedding presents and shut yourself up in your room to cry and wait here to make cow-eyes at your former lover when he comes back!'

'He *wasn't* my—' She bit it off, and glared at him. 'I couldn't possibly come tonight anyway, not with all the clearing up to do, so why suggest it?'

'Of course you could—if you dare. Your mother's just going to put her feet up while the caterers do all the clearing away, so what does she need you for? I suppose,' he said scornfully, 'that you haven't got the courage to leave, so I don't know why I'm wasting my breath! But that's what it is, a bloody waste!'

'All right, I'll come!' Vicky flung it at him, and she could hear the goaded note in her own voice. 'But only if you can really offer me work straight away. And you can pay me agency rates while I decide if I like it. If I don't, I'll stay in London and look for another job instead! I'm not signing any contracts until I know what I'm getting into, and if you're really willing to drive me back with you tonight you'll have to wait until *I'm* ready to go! Clear?'

'Quite clear. You're a practical little lady, Miss Vicky Jardine.'

He held out his hand to her, the gesture of a pact sealed, and she found herself putting her own hand into his. Heavens, she thought wildly, what on earth would her parents say to her taking off after the wedding with one of Marina's friends, and such a noticeably attractive one at that, just as if . . . She pulled her hand hastily out of the warm clasp of his with the hazy feeling that the handshake really had sealed something, so she couldn't back out now. She looked up at him curiously, with a confusion which didn't only come from the unexpected change in her future.

'You really are impulsive, aren't you? You don't know anything about me!'

'Yes to the first. Not true, the second. Observation tells a great deal. Besides, if you're a lousy nurse, I'll sack you.'

'I'm not a lousy nurse. You can be a good one without training in London, or do you only go for snob appeal? We ought to go back,' Vicky said with dignity, suddenly all too aware that her tart answer had been outright rudeness. But then, he had been consistently rude to her, hadn't he? She stole a glance up at him, but he was only looking amused. 'We've been out here for ages, and Marina must be almost ready to go away, I should think.'

'Yes I suppose we'd better move. Here, have a handkerchief—though I think those tears have dried by now, haven't they?' He *would* have to remind her of them, and study her like that as if it was his job to check that she looked presentable—but she accepted the handkerchief. 'Don't scrub with it, I don't want it covered with make-up!' he added.

Definitely a man who was used to lending his handkerchief to females. Well, she wouldn't have thought he was

anything else but used to the company of women. They
probably gathered round him like moths. Vicky, whose
clear translucent skin needed little make-up anyway,
dabbed her face carefully, then wiped her green-stained
hands thoroughly on his clean white cotton square before handing it back to him. The fence was always mossy
and she knew perfectly well how hard she'd been clutch-
ing it. He gave her another amused look, wiped his own
hands, dusted his sleeve, and turned to stroll back with
her.

Vicky, suddenly remembering something and wanting
to break the silence, said, 'I think I'm probably expected
to stay for the party. All the younger relations are
supposed to be going.'

'Well, if you can't get out of it, I'll have to come too,
won't I? Now that we're partners,' Simon said smoothly,
'we can console each other, can't we?'

'Thanks, but I don't propose to be that much of a
second-best!' Even as she said it, Vicky marvelled to
hear herself talking to a man like this in such a way. She
seemed to be behaving quite contrarily to her usual
nature.

Why she should be expected to like him after all he'd
said to her, Vicky couldn't think. She cast an uncertain
glance at him, and saw that he was looking amused
again. He really was extraordinarily changeable. They
were coming out through the shrubbery now, into full
view of anyone who happened to be looking, and unexpectedly he reached for her hand, caught it, gave it a
little pinch and went on holding it. 'Look, they're all
flooding out that way, the bride and groom must be on
the point of going away. Cheer up—if Marina throws her
bouquet to you, *I'll* catch it, and that should really put
her off her honeymoon!'

She couldn't think of any answer to that, particularly
not when they were suddenly in amongst a bunch of
other guests. She was feeling confused by his sudden

attack of telepathy anyway. How had he known that as soon as he said 'going away' she had felt a sudden dread that Marina really would throw the bridal bouquet directly at her, in sweet sisterly ignorance? She kept a defiant hold on Simon's hand, not caring what anybody made of it, particularly not the aunts who, if they noticed, would be cooing that 'dear little Victoria had found herself a boyfriend'. Some boyfriend, if they only knew! But she realised abruptly, and with surprise, that she had been far too angry during the past half-hour to be miserable. Was that part of his intention? No, she would not start thinking he was kind when he so obviously wasn't. Deep in thought, for a moment she barely noticed Marina coming out of the house with Andrew behind her. They were soon climbing into the car and waving and having confetti thrown at them, and because Vicky was near the back of the crowd Marina didn't see her and threw her bouquet to someone else. The happy couple drove off in a spurt of gravel and to cheers. Someone nearby said, 'Where are they going, does anyone know?'

Someone else answered, 'Venice, wasn't it? Mmm, all that romance, and gondolas!'

'What a stupid place to go in high summer. The canals will stink and the gondolas are all motorised nowadays.' It was Simon's voice, drawling softly just above Vicky's head, his scornful comment for her ears alone. She turned to give him a look—had he thought she might weaken into tears again, and lapse into romantic grief at the mention of Venice?—but he merely raised an ironic eyebrow at her. People were drifting back towards the house and the marquee entrance in search of more champagne—or perhaps even tea, an idea which struck Vicky with a sudden mundane yearning so strong that she almost wanted to laugh.

'What time is it?' she asked Simon.

'Mm? Almost six.' Inspecting his watch made him let

go of her hand, and he didn't bother to take it again. Well, he wouldn't now that Marina wasn't there to notice. 'When do you think you'll be able to get away?'

'I don't know. You'll just have to wait and see, won't you? It was *your* idea,' she said defensively. 'And anyway, even if we don't go to the party, I've got to see the parents and pack. Oh, do you want me to bring my uniforms?'

'You can, if that's what you prefer to wear. We have white overalls, all sizes. If you decide to stay you can have some of your own made, if you like it better that way. Disposable paper caps—unless you have something particular and frilly that you can't bear not to wear!'

'No, I haven't.' Suddenly it seemed frighteningly real. She was going to take off into the unknown with Simon Harraday, Marina's ex-boyfriend, a virtual stranger who had flung her the offer of a job on impulse and might even now be regretting it. He didn't look as if he was regretting it. He was giving her one of his mocking looks again, as if he thought she was such a spineless little coward she'd back out. 'Paper caps will be fine, thank you,' Vicky told him firmly. 'You'd better come and meet my parents, I suppose—well, I've got to tell them where I'm going, haven't I!'

But what on earth her parents would say at finding their quiet younger daughter behaving so uncharacteristically as to take off for London with one of the wedding guests, she couldn't imagine.

CHAPTER TWO

THE PARENTS said very little. Perhaps it was Simon's air of charming apology as he explained that he had persuaded Vicky to help him out in a staffing crisis which made the whole thing pass off so naturally. Or perhaps it was the fact that the two doctors took an instant liking to one another and lapsed at once into talking shop. It was left to Vicky's mother to say mildly, 'But darling, don't you need your holiday?' However, as a doctor's wife Mrs Jardine was used to putting medical necessities first, so she merely told Vicky where to find a suitably large suitcase and reminded her that one of her uniform dresses was washed but not ironed. They decided to stay for a light snack supper but it was agreed that they should skip the extra festivities.

Dr Jardine seemed to know Simon's name even if Vicky hadn't, and once all the relatives were out of the way the two doctors got deep into a discussion of the right age for a hip-fracture to be properly reduced and a replacement joint fitted—Dr Jardine had a case at the moment involving a local farm-labourer's daughter who had fallen from a barn roof. Eventually Mrs Jardine gave her younger daughter a resigned smile across the table and broke into the discussion to point out that it was half-past eight. Somehow there had been no chance for anything other than the lightest comments about how well the wedding had gone and how nice it was to see all the relatives—but even nicer that they hadn't wanted to stay on through the evening. Then Vicky was giving both parents a hug and climbing into Simon's car.

It was a Porsche, dark, low-slung and powerful—just the sort of car she might have expected him to have. The

seats were pushed back so far to accommodate his long
legs that Vicky felt several miles away from the dash-
board, but it was remarkably comfortable once she had
got used to feeling so low on the road and had reminded
herself that the seat-belt held her firmly so she needn't
clutch at the doorstrap for safety.

He was a fast driver, but a good one. Once out of the
twisty lanes and onto dual-carriageway, then motorway,
she felt the car leap into power like a great unleashed
cat, although the speedometer needle stayed flickering
on the legal seventy. He was a silent driver, too. Vicky
would have expected to feel awkward, shut up with him
in this small space, but being ignored while he concentrated was somehow restful. The day fell away behind
her with the miles. She didn't need to think about it, nor
about this unreal journey with a different life at the end
of it.

What would London be like? She had never imagined
herself living there, but she felt a stir of excitement. It
was the centre of everything and it was somehow ridiculous that she had never taken the trouble to go there in
all her twenty-three years except for one brief visit as a
child. She remembered only the hugeness of the buildings and the bewildering bright acres of shops—but that
was a child's-eye view. Now it occurred to her that it had
the National Theatre and art galleries and concert halls,
and she could get her fill of culture if she wanted to by
going round all of them in her time off. She could even
go back to the Tower of London and see if the Crown
Jewels were as huge and shiny as she vaguely remembered them—though truth to tell she didn't remember
them much, because she had been more impressed by
some sailing boat moored at the riverside, and had spent
a long time keeping her eyes fixed on Tower Bridge
because she couldn't believe it ever really opened.

She stole a glance at Simon, aware that he would find
her thoughts childish. London wasn't exciting to him. It

was just the place where he lived and worked. He was part of it. He'd probably be shocked if he knew just how much of a country girl he'd kidnapped. Not that she was totally unsophisticated, Vicky reminded herself, one could hardly get through nursing training and remain naive. New towns, with their population of resettled city dwellers, had their share of the sleazier side of urban life—muggings and youth gangs included. But London! There was a thrill about London, about its vast size and endless pavements and constant life, the sense of being alive at the very heart of things amongst millions of other people. Anything might happen in London. Vicky had to restrain a sudden nervousness that she'd get lost—she could always buy a street map. And if she got homesick for the country, she could go and sit in one of the parks.

Simon flicked his headlights on and as if reminded of her presence, said, 'Music?' and turned the radio knob without waiting for her to answer. There was a chatter of static as he fiddled, then something lightly classical with a piano sending fluid cascades of notes out of stereo speakers behind the seats. Violins smoothed in, melodic but unsentimental. Vicky turned her head to look at Simon again, seeing his profile still clear against the slowly gathering dusk, and making a surreptitious study of the triangular face, winged eyebrows, heavy-lidded dark eyes. What an unlikely companion he was for her, with his tidy, self-sufficient, arrogant good looks. And why did she suddenly feel half-excited, half-afraid? When he spoke she jumped guiltily, sure that he must have felt her scrutiny and perhaps read her mind as well, but he only said, 'D'you want to tune it to something else?'

'What? Oh—no, thanks. It's very pleasant.'

'Nice and soothing for driving to. But I can stand disc-jockey chatter if you prefer it. Just twiddle that knob there if you decide you want a change.'

She shook her head, then realised he wouldn't see it.

The music lapped round them, creating an odd sense of intimacy. Vicky felt a peculiar tingling sensation which started at the back of her neck and ran down both her arms and she found herself wriggling her toes as if sure they were going to be affected next. She felt fizzy and strange, but that must be because she was tired, still overwrought after the past few weeks and now excited about London too. And maybe her neck was tingling because she'd screwed her long hair up too tightly on to her head when she hastily did it for the journey, brushing it out quickly and roughly from its more elaborate bridesmaid's style. It had to be something mundane which was making her feel electrical quivers along her skin and an odd sense of breathlessness—*of course*, it had nothing to do with the velvety quality in Simon's deep voice, which she couldn't help noticing whenever he spoke. It fitted his appearance so well. It didn't fit his personality though, Vicky reminded herself, because that was far more abrasive. And she'd better remember, if ever she was in danger of forgetting it, that he'd collected her up because she was useful, and for no other reason. She stirred a little, realising that she didn't actually know her exact destination and 'London' covered a lot of ground.

'Where exactly is your clinic?'

'Cranshaw Street. Two streets away from Wimpole Street.'

She'd heard of Wimpole Street but that didn't get her much further, though she didn't feel inclined to tell him so in case her ignorance seemed babyish. Instead she asked, 'Do you have your consulting rooms there too?'

'Not in the same building, no. I've got rooms just round the corner. Handy enough, and better not to mix up consultations and admissions.' He added, 'Motorway driving's boring I'm afraid, but at least it's fast. Are you reasonably comfortable?'

'Yes, thanks.' In fact there was something strangely

relaxed and dreamlike about leaning back comfortably in this small space, the music weaving in and out of the powerful hum of the engine, the low roof closing them in . . . Vicky turned her head hastily to stare out at the gathering dark beyond the window, feeling stupidly confused by the drift of her own thoughts. Just because she was *with* him didn't mean they were *together*. It was a muddled thought but one which served to remind her that she was here because of loving and losing Andrew, because the hole left in her life by the loss of his dear familiarity was so unbearable that her only hope was to fill it up with work. That was what she was doing here. She certainly wasn't planning to fill the hole by feeling drawn to Simon Harraday, so much Andrew's opposite in looks and behaviour—the idea was ridiculous, because he definitely wasn't her type. And just as well, since she quite certainly wasn't his, any more than in the end she'd been Andrew's. She bit her lip, suddenly afraid that weariness and heartbreak would overwhelm her.

Out of the dimness she heard Simon say, 'Oh, by the way, remind me to send your father that article out of the BMJ we were talking about, will you?'

It was an impersonal comment, casually delivered, so there was no reason why it should bring that sense of intimacy back again between them, yet somehow it did. Vicky swallowed, felt glad he didn't seem to expect an answer, and leaned forward quickly to twiddle the radio knob. After all, he'd said she could change it if she wanted to. He didn't make any objection to the news bulletin she found and didn't comment, either, when she followed it up by listening intently to a summing-up of the situation in the Middle East, which was, as usual, complicated enough to require her complete concentration. At least, she thought she was concentrating, though she kept missing bits as the announcer's voice blurred against the hypnotic effect of headlights

approaching and receding along the dark endlessness of
the road . . .

She woke with a jerk to find they were amongst
streets. Wide streets, heavily built up, with long terraces
of shop-fronts which looked slightly scruffy and dust-
laden under the orange flare of street lights. Several sets
of traffic-lights later, Simon turned off into smarter,
tree-lined streets and then into a maze of squares with
tall Georgian terraces of houses and central gardens. He
was still driving with the same quiet, relaxed concentration, and Vicky felt guiltily that he must be tired by now
too, and perhaps she ought to have been entertaining
him.

He saw she was awake and said, 'Almost there,' with
an easiness which again didn't require her to answer,
though a moment later he added, with a touch of approval, 'You're a nice restful companion, I must say. I'm glad
you're not a smoker—though I should think you've seen
too many chronic bronchitics to be tempted, haven't
you?'

'I never started. Well, apart from trying one once
behind the bicycle shed at school, for rebellion's sake,
and I didn't like it much!' She heard her voice sounding
shy and husky with sleep. 'Actually no one in the family
smoked, except Marina.'

'Who had the sense to stop by the time she got into
medical school. No, its not one of my vices, either.' She
felt him glance at her. Was it because they'd both
noticed her tiny pause when she said her sister's name?
But his voice was lazily amused as he went on. 'What else
did you get up to behind the bicycle shed, I wonder? Or
is that too obvious a question? You're saved from
answering, anyway—we're here.'

It was an ordinary street, quite narrow, pavemented,
and set with the occasional tree. The streetlamps here
were white not orange, and quite widely-spread so that
there were pools of shadow between. It looked like a

residential area rather than a place where one would find a children's hospital, even a small one. Vicky struggled out of her seat-belt and tried to feel alert, ready to face the peculiarity of arriving at a totally new place of work in the middle of the night. Not, of course, that she'd be expected to work tonight, but she couldn't help feeling that it was still an odd time to turn up unannounced. Somehow she hadn't thought about that, it just hadn't come up. But perhaps Simon made a habit out of collecting up stray nurses from around the countryside and dumping them at his clinic at odd hours. She looked dubiously around at the narrow town houses with neatly-painted front doors and brass knockers glintingly polished, and window-boxes with their bright flowers washed to neutrality by the artificial light. None of the houses actually looked large enough to contain a clinic, but perhaps it was adapted out of several put together. She was conscious all over again of Simon's height as he led her towards a door, with her suitcase dangling from his hand, and his other casually under her elbow. She wished she didn't feel dwarfed into insignificance. She wished too that she felt properly awake, so that she could appreciate the fact that she was really here, in London, starting a new life. He opened the door with a key, and pointed her towards a carpeted flight of stairs straight ahead, switching on a light as he did so and saying, 'Up', with the minimum of information, which seemed to be habitual to him.

She went up. Later, she would notice that the carpet was pale green and the walls papered in a pale Regency stripe, though at the moment she was too dazed to take in her surroundings with any particularity. The stairs let to a small landing and a white-painted door, which opened on to what was plainly a sitting-room. A settee, two chintz-covered armchairs, more of the pale green carpet. Two well-proportioned windows let in a filtering of the street lights outside before Simon went to draw the curtains across them, having flicked a switch which lit both central light and shaded lamps set on a polished table and a desk. It was neither a masculine room nor a feminine one, merely pleasant and comfortable-looking. Vicky looked round her uncertainly. There was nobody around, and no sound of anyone either, though there were two further doors leading off the sitting room and the glimpse of a further flight of stairs, too, leading away upwards.

'Where—?'

'Is your bedroom? Up the stairs there. I'll show you in a minute. The bathroom's up there too, in between the two bedrooms on that floor. Apart from that, there's a kitchen—' he pointed at one of the two doors, 'my bedroom,' he pointed at the other, 'and downstairs there's a dining-room, too far from the kitchen to be practical so it doesn't get used as such, and a cloakroom, and a back door out to the garden. And this is the sitting-room, as you can see. The garden's pretty small, but you can hang washing in it—though not out of the front windows, because there's a by-law. Now—'

'But this isn't the clinic!'

'No, of course it isn't. I wasn't expecting you to start work tonight. Good heavens, you did think I was a slave-driver, didn't you!' He raised an amused eyebrow at her, standing in the middle of the room looking nonchalant and overwhelmingly good-looking and not at all as if he had just spent several hours driving. 'There wouldn't be anywhere for you to sleep there. It isn't residential for the nursing staff. This, fairly obviously, is where I live. You haven't got anywhere else to stay in London, have you?'

'Who—who else lives here?'

'No one else at the moment. Of recent date I've had the place to myself. There's plenty of room, so you might as well move in here. So, come on, let's go and make up your bed.'

'But I can't possibly sleep—'

Vicky broke off, because he had straightened up from bending down to pick up her suitcase and was looking at her with a distinct glint in his eye, though also with a look of amusement.

'I wasn't suggesting we shared it, you know!'

'No, that wasn't what I meant! I just—I meant—if you're living here on your own, I can't possibly stay here!'

'Good God, girl, what century have you been living in? People share mixed-sex accommodation all the time nowadays, or haven't you noticed? With or without the . . . fringe benefits.' He was giving her a positively evil grin. 'I'm not at all against the fringe benefits if you're not, but you needn't worry that I'll assault you—unless of course I get an invitation. I like my women willing. Mind you,' his eyes ran over her with a lingering emphasis, 'you do make rather an appealing picture standing there all pink-cheeked and big-eyed. No, all right, you're too tired to be teased, aren't you? But you really are an original, Vicky Jardine, and I do find that almost irresistible!'

'I merely meant,' Vicky told him in a shaking voice, which was part embarrassment but even more a confused anger at his sudden kindly condescension, 'that if you're living here on your own, you'd find it inconvenient to have me to stay! And besides, it would be awkward, when I'm working for you, wouldn't it?'

'No, not at all, I can give you a lift to work in the mornings.'

'But—' No, she wasn't going to ask him what the other nurses at the clinic would think about it, because that would make him start mocking her all over again. 'You said somebody else usually shares with you. Or did share with you. What if they suddenly want to come back?'

'Not very likely, just at the moment. Any more objections?'

In the face of that sardonically raised eyebrow she could hardly blurt out that he was far too—far too *everything* for her to feel comfortable living under the same roof as him. Besides, it was his roof, and she supposed it was kind of him to suggest it. She couldn't very well go out and walk the streets looking for somewhere else to live at this time of night, even if she'd known where to start looking. 'What happens,' she asked tartly, 'when you want to fill the house with willing females? I mean, it won't exactly be convenient for you having me here then, will it?'

'When I do, I'll ask you to go out. And when you want to fill the house with willing males, you can ask me to go out.' He was looking highly amused. 'I'm sure we'll come to some reasonable arrangement! Now, shall we go and look for those bedclothes? I could try and find a key for your bedroom door as well, if it'd make you feel better—though of course, you could never be sure I hadn't got a spare!'

'If I was that worried, I'd put a chair under the doorhandle,' Vicky retorted, stung by his open mockery into answering back.

'Better. Certainly better. Come on, I'm tired, even if you aren't. Don't let me forget to give you a front door key in the morning . . . Oh, do you want anything to eat or drink? I seem to have had enough today, but—'

'No. Thank you.'

He picked her suitcase up again and led the way. The top floor was compact, just a tiny landing and three doors. He opened one to show her a modern fitted bathroom and pulled some sheets out of an airing-cupboard just inside it, then led the way into the bedroom. It was small but pleasant, with a window out on to the street, though it wouldn't be noisy, he said, if she ever needed to sleep after a night-duty. Hearing him say that made her look round with a feeling of unreality. Was she really going to live here? But while she was still

gazing blankly round at the comfortable-looking bed
and the pleasant, quietly-patterned wallpaper he had
gone to do a quick check on the chest of drawers to make
sure it was empty. A similar check on the wardrobe
made him frown and he swept a couple of dresses off
hangers, murmuring that he didn't know how *those* got
left in here. They were the kind of clothes Marina
wore—and Vicky felt a sudden sharp realisation. Someone had just moved out, he had said so. Had Marina
actually been living with him? She could scarcely ask him
outright, but it suddenly seemed likely, particularly after
some of the things he'd said this afternoon. And of
course that betraying, 'It's surprising Simon came to the
wedding, of all people,' which she had overheard without, then, understanding. Marina, Simon's girlfriend.
Marina in residence. Marina radiantly off on honeymoon with Andrew, now . . .

She found she was assuring Simon that she could make
up the bed by herself, thank you. And then his tall figure
was filling the doorway and he was saying a light, slightly
mocking, 'Sleep well then, if you've got everything you
want.' And then he was gone. Dazed though she felt, she
had better unpack at least one of her uniform dresses
and hang it up to let the creases drop out. She had better
at least *try* to feel that all this was really happening.

Some time later, lying in bed, she found that lying
down seemed only to make her more wakeful. It wasn't
that the wedding was playing itself back inside her head,
because she refused to let it—though the tension of *not*
letting all the jumbled memories of today flood in didn't
help her to relax. She wasn't thinking about Marina and
Andrew wherever they were now, either. That would
have been both an intrusion and the sort of self-inflicted
torture which would have made her the deliberate mar-
tyr Simon had accused her of being. Simon . . . she tried
to blank him out too, though not before she had thought
that he had no right to fling those accusations at her

when he had chosen to come to the wedding and watch
the girl he'd been living with get married to someone
else. She wasn't going to pretend to herself that when
Marina had been living here, she and Simon had necessarily slept at opposite ends of the house. She might be
the stay-at-home sister, but she wasn't entirely ignorant
of the modern world. Vicky tossed uncomfortably, remembering how Marina had always got any boyfriend
she wanted. She had never seemed to want any of them
permanently, though, until she met Andrew. Andrew!
She was not going to let herself think about him!

She couldn't sleep because it was all so unfamiliar. If
only she hadn't dropped off in the car, she might be
sleepy as well as tired now. Lying in bed with her eyes
wide open was stupid, because it made her aware of the
street light coming in from the window where she'd
pulled the curtains apart. She could see the unfamiliar
shape of the room, reminding her that she wasn't where
she usually was, at home. London, she was in London. It
was surprisingly quiet here for a city. She would have
expected to hear the distant grind of traffic all the time.
Vicky closed her eyes, opened them again, wondered
irritably whether to get up and close the curtains, then
decided not to because she was afraid of not waking
early enough in the morning. Her long, thick hair felt
heavy and hot around her neck—she should have plaited
it to keep it out of the way, instead of just pulling all the
pins out and letting it hang in its loose curtain. Perhaps
she'd have it all cut off as a mark of her new London
personality, and wear it short and curly, the way Marina
did hers . . . No, not like Marina's because Simon would
undoubtedly notice and make some mocking comment if
she did that! She wondered why he wasn't married. If
he'd been two years ahead of Marina in training, that
meant he must be what, twenty-nine? Well, he didn't
have to be married, after all. Perhaps he didn't believe in
it. Perhaps he hadn't got the girl he wanted. Somehow,

however, she couldn't imagine him not getting the girl he wanted, if he really chose to try.

It was no use lying here wondering why on earth she'd come. It had been a perfectly sensible thing to do. She was a good and efficient nurse and she knew it. Just because she'd stepped out of the tried and familiar paths, it didn't mean she wouldn't go on being a good nurse. She didn't have to feel just a little lost about the whole business, or find herself wishing she could walk back into her own ward tomorrow morning instead of into something so different. There was really no need for her to feel apprehensive, because sick children were sick children anywhere.

She realised abruptly that she probably couldn't sleep because she'd drunk too much champagne today, and without eating many of the snacks on offer. A glass of water might help to settle her. Better still, a glass of milk, if there was any. She lay still for a minute, then decided she *could* raid the kitchen, because after all she'd been hijacked here rather than being a polite guest. She scrambled out of bed and felt around for her dressing-gown. Simon must have gone to bed by now and she could remember clearly which door he'd said led to the kitchen. As long as she was quiet . . .

She crept down the stairs, sensing the softness of the carpet under her bare feet and trying not to feel a sudden, sharp homesickness. It was a feeling which came at her with a stab, and made her blink as she stepped out into the darkened sitting-room. Or perhaps it was the wide stripe of light across the floor which made her blink and try to readjust her eyes. The light must be coming in through one of the windows—no, surely the windows were the *other* side? She had stepped into the light before she realised that it came from an open door, and then she was staring straight in through the doorway at Simon, half-turned away from her. He was wearing only a dressing-gown in some dark, silky material, and was in the act of leaning forward to twitch a pillow into place on a bed.

He turned his head and saw her before she could move. For a second they stared at each other like a frozen tableau. Then Vicky said hesitantly, 'I couldn't get to sleep.'

She hadn't meant her voice to come out sounding small and lost. She wasn't aware that it did. She was only aware of Simon moving towards her on bare feet, with a strange expression on his face. Then he was pulling her into his arms, one hand tangling in her hair as he held her against him. She felt the warmth of his body through the thin silk, and the lean hardness of him. She felt his lips brush her forehead, then her cheek, then find her mouth with a sweetness which sent a sudden shiver all through her. It was like drowning, it was like . . .

Her lips parted under his and her hand stole up to touch his cheek, to slide up around his neck, to feel the silkiness of his hair, while her whole body seemed to come alive with sensations of almost unbearable yearning. Nothing had ever been like this. She had never experienced such strength and gentleness that her bones seemed to melt into his, and she wanted nothing so much as to cling even closer to him until she was lost entirely. When his lips slid away from hers she almost murmured in protest, but he was nuzzling them against her throat, sending ripples of pure animal delight through her as if her skin was suddenly sensitive all over.

She found that some distant, confused portion of her brain was wondering how anyone could ever *not* want to feel the strength of his arms holding her so tenderly— how could Marina ever . . .

She was abruptly rigid, her hands thrusting against his chest to push him away while her mouth uttered a violent, husky, strangled, '*No!*' No, she wasn't going to be a handy substitute for Marina, something more useful than those betraying clothes left behind in the wardrobe!

He must have relaxed his hold on her because she had put several feet between them almost before she'd realised how hard she'd sprung away from him. Her hands were spread out instinctively before her to ward him off, though he was standing still, his eyes a little unfocussed, breathing almost as hard as she was. Vicky gasped angrily, 'I didn't mean—I wasn't—I came down for a glass of water!'

'Really? You could have fooled me.' He was watching her, the sardonic twist coming back to his mouth. 'Do you always start something and then say no like that?' he asked savagely. 'One of these days you might get more than you bargained for!'

Vicky took a step backwards before she realised that he hadn't moved, but was merely watching her with a mocking look in his dark eyes. Mocking and angry, though his rapid breathing was going back to normal and he looked far more in control of himself than she felt. Vicky rubbed a hand across her mouth where it burned and stung. He must have taken the gesture for one of revulsion, because his eyes hardened. He opened his mouth to say something, but Vicky got in first.

'I didn't come down because I wanted to be—to be kissed! I am not one of your fringe benefits!'

'Then you shouldn't turn up at my bedroom door like an invitation! You could get a glass of water,' he said pointedly, 'out of the bathroom. Or are you going to pretend that you hadn't thought of that? Or say that there isn't a tooth-glass up there? Funny, there was one there half an hour ago! And for someone who doesn't want to be kissed,' he added nastily, between his teeth, 'you do it quite noticeably well! Or do you know that? Teases usually do!'

'I am not a—' Vicky glared at him. She was shaking inside, her emotions a jumble of fury, remembered delight and a bruising misery which made her feel as if she had been dropped down a lift shaft. 'You really are conceited,' she spat at him. 'You know perfectly well that I'm stupid enough to be in love with my sister's husband, and why on earth you think I should want *you* as a substitute I can't imagine! If you want to know, I came down for a glass of milk, and you certainly haven't got milk flowing out of the bathroom taps, have you? And if I can't even walk about at night without—'

'It won't happen again,' he said icily. 'There's the kitchen. Go on—and look for your milk!' And he turned on his heel, went into his bedroom and shut the door with a sharp click.

Vicky was trembling all over. She wanted to storm after him and say that she couldn't possibly stay here. Only the thought of his reaction if she burst into his bedroom after all that stopped her. She wanted to run away upstairs, too, shut herself in and bury her burning face against her pillow. But if she didn't go into the kitchen, he really would think . . .

She slammed her way across the room as noisily as possible, wrenched open the kitchen door, fumbled around for the light switch and made as much banging as she could as she opened up the fridge door. She was in a right royal rage. She was also, if she cared to examine it thoroughly, churningly miserable. How *dare* he kiss her like that and then call her a tease? Perhaps it might have looked odd, but what about his feelings for Marina? Vicky had a perfect right to feel insulted when he'd made it so clear that the other sister, who'd only recently moved out on him, was the one he really wanted, the one he would have preferred to have if only she was here. She gulped down a mug of cold milk far too fast, so that she almost choked. Then she slammed round the kitchen opening and shutting cupboard doors, until it occurred to her abruptly that if she went on, he might consider that was an invitation too. At the thought she went very quiet, closed everything up and crept back upstairs.

She couldn't possibly stay here after tomorrow. It was

going to be difficult enough to face him at breakfast.
And he hadn't even said what time he expected her to
have breakfast, or when he was going to take her to the
clinic. He hadn't said anything. In fact most of the times
he'd spoken to her since she met him, he'd merely been
horrible to her, taunting and mocking and making fun of
her feelings. He obviously thought she was thoroughly
boring. Except for the fact that she kissed 'noticeably
well'. No, she was not going to think about that! She
wasn't, either, going to acknowledge the edge of doubt
in her mind which made her realise that perhaps it had
looked as if she wanted him to kiss her. Well, she'd made
it clear enough now that she hadn't, and that ought to
have been a comfort. Except that it wasn't.

She was still shaking, and it didn't have much to do
with being angry. She had never felt quite like that
before, though she'd grown up with her share of local
boyfriends. Perhaps she would have felt this way if
Andrew had ever kissed her properly, instead of in his
friendly fashion on the cheek. She told herself that she
would have, of course, because she loved him, and that
made all the difference. Though *not* loving Simon
Harraday didn't seem to have mattered. But then Simon
had far too much of everything, including animal
magnetism.

No, she couldn't possibly live here. It was an impossible situation, quite unsuitable for her to live in his house
when she was working for him. It made the wrong
relationship. They didn't *have* a relationship. Except, of
course, for the fact that they were both of them somebody's 'ex'.

From Simon's point of view, he obviously wouldn't go
on being anybody's 'ex' for long. He wasn't the type.
There would soon be another tall, beautiful girl taking
up his time. And then Vicky would have to move out
anyway—which would certainly be safer.

She didn't meditate on the 'safer'. She had thought

her tangled emotions would keep her awake, but instead they seemed to have exhausted her, and she slept. And on the edge of sleep, it somehow didn't seem peculiar that she had gone back to wondering, cloudily, how on earth Marina came to give someone like Simon Harraday up.

CHAPTER THREE

SHE DIDN'T oversleep because Simon banged on her door, and shouted 'Time to get up,' loudly enough to wake anyone. When she went into the bathroom Vicky found a note scrawled in large black capital letters propped against the basin saying, 'Beware, variable water temperatures in shower.' For a moment she wondered uneasily whether he'd decided to communicate with her by notes from now on, but sense reasserted itself as she realised that it was merely a practical warning. Last night's confrontation seemed unreal, anyway. She had woken wondering whether she'd actually dreamed it.

She dressed quickly in her familiar blue-striped uniform dress, cinching the silver-buckled belt tightly round her waist, and pinning her SRN badge on to her top pocket. It made her feel better, more like her real self, to be in uniform. She coiled her hair up carefully and pinned it in place. It reached almost to her waist, thick and straight and shiny, so that it took some anchoring to make sure it would stay firmly up all through a working day. Then she went downstairs trying to feel cool and efficient to match her appearance, instead of nervous and faintly wary.

The kitchen was cheerful and full of the sun. It was a small room, so it was also full of Simon. He was sitting at the central table with his top half invisible behind a Sunday paper and the remains of breakfast spread out on the table in front of him. He had obviously beaten her to it by quite some time. Vicky had completely forgotten it was Sunday and thought hazily that that might explain why everywhere still seemed so quiet for the middle of a city. She also wondered uncertainly whether she'd been right to come down in her uniform—had he meant her to start work tomorrow, not today? But, after all, hospitals did function seven days a week, three-hundred-and-sixty-five days a year, night as well as day. Simon certainly didn't make any comment as he glanced round the edge of his paper at her arrival, returned behind it, and said,

'Hunt around for whatever you want to eat. There's eggs, cereal, bread. Tea or coffee, and the kettle's over there beside the cooker.'

He obviously intended her to make herself at home, and didn't seem to expect her to say anything polite like 'Good morning.' Vicky edged her way round him trying not to feel self-conscious. There was far too much of him in this small space for her not to feel thoroughly aware of him, even if he had been the sort of person one could ever not be aware of, but Vicky busied herself finding a cup and saucer and warming up the electric grill to make toast, trying to be unobtrusive and not bump into his chair. A surreptitious glance at him showed him looking tidy, shaven, and formal for a Sunday in a shirt and tie, so presumably he planned to be on duty himself at the clinic today. She wondered uncomfortably whether she had imagined a sour note in his voce. Was he the sort of person who was always moody at breakfast, or was she supposed to make something out of being so thoroughly ignored? She kept her back firmly to him while she watched her toast, because standing at the cooker brought her round his side of the newspaper. She felt as if the silence was stretching her nerves. After a moment, still carefully not looking at him she said, 'About my living here—'

There was a sharp rustle of newspaper behind her. 'I said it wouldn't happen again,' Simon said curtly, and then, 'For goodness' sake, girl, don't sulk!'

'I'm not!' Vicky rescued her toast with a carefully

controlled movement that gave her time to put what she hoped was a note of polite surprise into her voice. '*I'm* not sulking!'

'Aren't you?' His eyes were waiting to mock her as she turned round. 'Well I'm not, with just as much cause! I'm sitting here quietly reading the paper in peace—or I was. I never talk at breakfast time. You'd better get used to it.'

'All the same, it would probably be better—'

'All right! Just this once! I won't apologise for kissing you, but I'll apologise for what I said afterwards. Does that satisfy you? Now can we drop the subject, instead of making a meal out of it? All that icy dignity is too much first thing in the morning. Eat your toast, and have the colour supplement.'

'I didn't raise the subject,' Vicky told him, aware that her cheeks were flaming, but she added for good measure and with some of the dignity of which he'd already accused her, 'I just don't like misunderstandings, that's all.'

'Yes, I did gather that's what it was. Of course, if you'd really like to discuss it—'

'No, you're quite right, let's drop the subject.' The edge of amused mockery in his voice sent Vicky into a brisk action and she sat down hastily and picked up the colour supplement he had offered her. The only thing to do was to be official. 'What time do you want to leave? Oh, and while I am here, I'd better pay you rent, hadn't I? I'm not exactly a house-guest. You'll have to tell me how much.'

'Yes, all right, we'll sort something out. And about food, too, because we won't always be in at the same hours. Damn that phone.' It was ringing in the sitting-room, and he unwound himself from his chair to go and answer it. Against its insistent ring she heard him say, behind her, 'I'm sure we can work out some way of living in comparative peace. You should remember that

I'm only human, but I don't carry quarrels over until morning.'

Since he was already picking up the phone, that gave him the last word. Vicky took a large bite out of her toast, and tried not to listen. It was impossible not to hear what he was saying, however, for his voice carried too clearly. 'No, she's not here, I'm afraid. She left about ten days ago. Didn't she tell you? Oh, I see, you've been away. No, I'm afraid I can't give you her address, she's abroad and I don't know it. Okay then.'

Vicky heard the ping as the receiver went back on its rest and stiffened a little, but he remained next door and she could hear him opening and shutting drawers. It had given her a faint feeling of shock to hear his words, and she supposed, with some bitterness, that she really was something of an innocent. Marina had been engaged to Andrew for six weeks. And she had only moved out of here ten days ago . . . She wondered why Simon hadn't said bluntly, 'She's married,' but she supposed he didn't want whoever it was at the other end to start making sympathetic noises. He obviously had his defences too.

She was washing up by the time he came back into the kitchen. Tidiness was automatic after ward work, so she was surprised when he seemed pleased to find the table neatly cleared and the things put away in what probably weren't their proper places. As she dried her hands, he held out a Yale key for her, saying, 'Front door, don't lose it. Back door's on a mortice lock, but you can't come in that way anyway. Unfortunately there's no back entrance to the garden, which means nowhere to put a garage, either. Still, there were enough other advantages to make the place worth buying.'

'It's your own house?'

'Yes—leasehold, of course. You can't buy freehold property in central London because most of it belongs to the Duke of Westminster and gets sold only on ninety-nine year leases. This one's got . . . oh, sixty-six to go, so

I should think it should see me out!' He was chatting absently, frowning out at the tiny walled garden below, which Vicky had already peered down at across the sink. It wasn't really a garden because it was mainly paved, with a small strip of grass and some undistinguished bushes. Beyond its high end wall she had glimpsed another similar garden but with more grass and with a child's swing in it, backing onto a similar house which, like this one, was part of a neat terrace. She had wondered a little at the broken glass which topped all the garden walls as far as she could see and struck her as faintly sinister. She glanced up at Simon. Talking about property was at least a safe subject.

'Why all the glass?'

'Mm? Oh—it's not anti-neighbour, it's anti-burglar. I suppose I ought to remind you not to open the door at night without putting the chain on. It's only a precaution, but better if you're alone in the house. Oh, and take a taxi back if you've been working late—yes, even round here!'

'You make it sound . . . Well, I suppose it's the same anywhere nowadays, isn't it?' Except in a village where you knew everyone. Vicky ignored her faint flicker of homesickness, crushing it down in favour of a sense of adventure—though it occurred to her that if she did look for somewhere else to live she'd better take care to choose something in a respectable area. It was odd and disorientating to realise how much she was on her own. It made her feel a little less certain about leaving Simon's protective aura—though protective wasn't exactly the right word to have chosen, however much he might have sounded it just now. She glanced up at him, and said staunchly, 'Did you know that Birmingham's as violent as London, and Glasgow's more violent than either? When did you say you wanted to go?'

'Now, if you're ready.' He snapped back to attention and turned away from the window, slanting a smile at

her which was purely amiable. 'Sister should be glad to
see you. I'll suggest she puts you on to watching and
finding your way around, today—but she runs all that
side of things, I don't!'

Vicky went down the stairs ahead of him. Outside, the
street looked much as it had last night, but brighter, lit
by the morning sun. The Porsche stood where they had
left it. Other cars parked along the street were similarly
sleek-looking—no shabby family saloons here—and
Vicky decided that the burglar precautions must have
been put up with good reason, because this was obviously a smart area. She decided too that Simon must be
doing well in his private practice if he could afford to buy
a house in a street like this. He looked too smooth to be
anything but successful, anyway.

She was just thinking about that while he opened up
the car, when a girl in a jogging suit emerged from a door
opposite, called out cheerfully, 'Morning, Si!' and loped
purposefully off down the street. She was tall, slender,
ash blonde, and very beautiful, with a racehorse elegance which was apparent even through her grey
tracksuit.

'Morning, Chris! Neighbour,' Simon said explanatorily, pulling the Porsche door wide for Vicky to climb
in. Vicky, scrambling in obediently, caught herself
thinking that with neighbours like that, he really
wouldn't have to be broken-hearted for long. She also
wondered whether the other girl's interested glance in
her direction had meant anything. In the village it would
have spoken volumes. However, she wasn't going to
think about home and make herself more nervous.

It took a short ten minutes to reach the clinic and if
Vicky had hoped to watch the way there carefully, she
soon lost her bearings amongst the twists and turns
through the streets. Simon drew up outside a tall stone-
faced building in a wide street full of similar buildings. A
discreet brass plate beside double doors said simply,

'Harraday Clinic' and Simon led the way up the shallow flight of stone steps, whistling absently between his teeth. On his own familiar ground he was naturally at ease, and Vicky tried to hide her uncertainty as he held the door open for her to pass him. Once inside, however, it was less unfamiliar, because in spite of an elegant arrangement of flowers on a table just inside the door there was that faint, indefinable feel of a hospital about the place, familiar to anyone who had worked in one. A compound of floor-polish and pine disinfectant and starch in the air, the click of heels on a linoleum floor, glass swing doors ahead wide enough to take a stretcher or a wheelchair. Simon led her past a door marked Secretary's Office and another one marked Waiting Room and through the glass doors, where the passage-way promptly angled and had doors either side of it painted in bright pastel colours.

He stopped beside the nearest open door, and everything became even more familiar because the door was marked Sister-in-Charge and the room looked like any sister's office anywhere. Behind a desk a slim, grey-haired woman in sister's uniform and frilly-edged cap looked up quickly from some notes she was writing, and smiled.

'You're in, are you? I thought you had the whole weekend off—I suppose I should have known better!' The words were addressed to Simon, in a slightly motherly tone which was both thoroughly informal, and surprising. 'I haven't got any special worries for you, but you're going to go round I suppose?'

'I promised I'd bring Jonas another car. One that wouldn't break if it was trodden on.' Simon was grinning broadly, and he dug in his pocket to produce a small, bright green, metallic version of his own Porsche. 'Will it do, d'you think? Best I could find, and the doors open. This is Vicky Jardine, Sister, and I've snatched her off a children's ward where she was a staff nurse. She liked the idea of coming to London, so I said we'd put her on the same payroll as the agency staff while she was finding her feet. I'll leave the rest to you.'

His tall figure removed itself from beside Vicky and vanished along the corridor. She was left facing Sister—aware of a swift assessing glance, and then a smile as the woman rose to her feet.

'He'll spoil that child, and one of these days I'll tell him that he only buys him cars because he likes playing with them himself! Well, Nurse Jardine. You're a nice surprise, I must say. Where have you come from, and how long can we have you for? Don't look so surprised—you've got that, which gives me an immediate feeling of security compared with having to work out what sort of training some of the agency nurses have had!' She was indicating Vicky's SRN badge. 'I hope Simon didn't actually snatch you! The way he feels about proper medicine, I wouldn't put anything past him.'

'No,' Vicky said shyly. Somehow it added reassuringly to the hospital atmosphere to find that he was 'Simon' to Sister while she was the more formal 'Sister' to him! 'I wanted a job in London, and he offered me one. I haven't got my P45 or anything, I'm afraid.'

'Oh, don't worry about that, you can deal with all that with the Bursar. We don't have a matron here either, just sisters-in-charge, with all the paperwork done by the secretarial side, thank goodness. Well, sit down, and tell me just what experience you have had. Clarice!' She called the name out abruptly, startling Vicky for a second, and a shadow which had just flashed past the door came back and turned into a busty blonde in a white overall with a cap perched on top of her curls. 'When are you off today?' Sister asked.

'One o'clock on the dot. Hi there,' Clarice said amiably to Vicky, giving her a friendly grin before she switched her attention back to Sister. She had a broad Australian accent, the sort Vicky thought turned up only

in films. 'The little lamb's dropped off at the moment,
Sister. He was crying a lot in the night, the night staff
said. Honestly, you'd think he'd have a granny who
could've taken him, wouldn't you?'

'His granny's in Sri Lanka, I think, making a
documentary about the position of women workers on
tea-plantations,' Sister said drily. 'And his other granny's in the Bahamas with her third husband. Or her
fourth. Did you get him to do his exercises before he
went to sleep?'

'Yeah. He was ever so good, bless him. Honestly, it
makes you spit,' Clarice said cheerfully. 'If you want me
to do something else, I can, until he wakes up. But not
after one o'clock, because that was a promise!'

'Yes, yes, I haven't forgotten.' Sister looked mildly
harassed and got up to look at a large chart pinned to
the wall. She didn't seem to mind Clarice's total informality of manner, and that was reassuring again. 'Who's
coming on with Paul after you? Oh yes, Beatrice, until
six. And then Lannie.'

'That's good, he likes having Lannie to put him to bed
for the night.'

'Does he?' Sister smiled. 'Lannie's from the Philip-
pines,' she told Vicky, 'SEN, but very useful. Right
then, Clarice, give me a few minutes with our new
recruit, and then you can show her round. I'll keep an
eye out down here while you show her everything upstairs. Paul will probably sleep for quite a while now he
has dropped off. How's his temperature this morning?'

'Up a bit, but it might be the crying. I'll come back in
ten minutes, then.'

Clarice shot away again after a grin at Vicky. Sister
returned to her chair. 'Paul's three, and not really ill,'
she explained, 'he caught German measles while he was
staying with a friend, and his mother couldn't have him
back because she's in early pregnancy. It's not the sort of
case we usually have because, obviously, we don't really

want a non-ill child with an infectious disease! However, we've got him down at the end on this floor, and thoroughly isolated.'

'Yes, Si—, Dr Harraday did mention something about it.'

'Did he? The mother's more brainless than I ought to mention, but then she does have her troubles. She lost her first baby, and there are Rhesus problems. Paul was born very slightly spastic. Very mild, so you wouldn't think it to look at him. But that's the real reason why we've got him, because he has to do a prescribed set of exercises every day if he isn't to grow up lame. But I needn't go into all that just now. Tell me about yourself.'

Vicky gave her qualifications and experience and was pleased to find that Sister showed interest in her training hospital. 'One of the shiny new ones! Lucky for you, they're building them with everything that opens and shuts nowadays!'

When asked, Vicky said that she was perfectly willing to work today. Sister said that she would put her on with someone for the afternoon shift, so that she could get used to things. Most of the small patients were acute rather than chronic, though one or two came in recurrently, such as an asthma case who had frighteningly severe bouts of the illness. Very few children were in the clinic for long, however, and never stayed more than a week or two unless there was some particular reason for it, like parents who had gone abroad. Vicky wondered how anyone could go abroad leaving a sick child behind. She reminded herself that there could be working mothers whose jobs took them away at the wrong moment, and perhaps for children who were used to being looked after by nannies and au pairs it wasn't quite so bad.

Clarice reappeared in the doorway, looking cheerful. Sister, whose name seemed to be Mary Cadogan according to a piece of plastic displayed on her desk, told them both to go away and start the conducted tour. She had already explained to Vicky that she alternated with another sister-in-charge, both of them the top staff members on the nursing side. There was another doctor, too, David Asscher who was Simon's assistant and part of the permanent staff. Visiting surgeons took care of operations in the clinic's top-floor theatre and brought their own team of theatre nurses with them, though a clinic nurse would also be there and act as the child's 'special' afterwards. It all seemed very well-organised, and well-equipped.

'I'm Clarice Bean, by the way. I didn't get your name?'

'Vicky Jardine.'

'Well, hi, Vicky. It's not at all bad working here, so I should stick with it. It pays a helluva lot better than hospitals—even back home.' Clarice delivered this cheerful comment over her shoulder as she led the way along the passage with its closed doors either side, then paused at the bottom of a wide flight of stairs. 'We'll go up first. I just took a peek at the little lamb and he's still fast-o. Anyway I can't take you in there because you'd have to gown up.'

'You're barrier-nursing him?'

'Yeah, seems a bit silly when it's just rubella, but we can't take the risk with any infection. That's why Sister put Lannie on with him as his sole nurse, because she just doesn't go anywhere else except with him, so he can see her properly instead of being faced with a sort of sinister bundle all the time. She's got the weekend off, though, till tonight.'

Clarice was leading the way upwards until they came out into another corridor, wider than the one downstairs. 'Let's take the lift up from here and start at the top. There aren't any ops today. You wouldn't catch a private surgeon working on a Sunday if he could help it—they'll all be out on the golf course! C'mon—here's the theatre lift. The one thing I don't like about this place is all the stairs!'

The lift, wide and deep enough to take a bed like all theatre lifts, carried them smoothly upwards. Vicky put questions in to Clarice's flow of chatter and found out that the ground floor, where she had seen Sister Cadogan, held mainly Sister's office and linen rooms and stores, plus a room for clinical examinations and a couple of extra rooms for patients, with their usual offices. It also held a kitchen, a nurses' rest room with, Clarice said, a buzzer in it which made it less restful, and a dining-room for staff to eat in during their duty hours. Duty hours, however, were usually organised to avoid meal times except during the night. There was another sister's office on the first floor, where the sister-in-charge was more usually found because it was nearer most of the patients. Sunday morning was a quiet time so Sister often used it for checking stores lists, and besides there was Paul down there at the moment with his usual 'special' off duty for the weekend.

Clarice ran through the information in a cheery stream. She was a large girl and looked as if she would be perennially good-tempered, with a direct, knowledge-able but bouncy manner which went with her bouncy blonde curls. She led Vicky efficiently around the top floor, showing her the two spotless operating theatres with an anaesthetic room each, the usual selection of cupboards for theatre equipment and a post-operative recovery room with its emergency trolleys and piped oxygen.

'Must have cost a few dollars to set this place up,' Clarice commented, and then caught herself up to add, 'Dollars, there I go again! I've been over here a year and I still forget it's pounds! Are you a Londoner?'

'No. English, but not London. In fact I haven't work-ed in London before.' Vicky smiled shyly at her companion as she answered the question. 'I was working until—

well, until this week—on a children's ward in Pensbury if you've ever heard of it!'

'Doesn't mean a thing,' Clarice said without rancour. 'I was a theatre nurse back home, but it's murder on the complexion after a while. Anyway, when I got engaged to Bill—that's my fella—I thought I'd jack it in. Didn't want to do night-time geriatrics either, though I tried it for a while, because it's what private nursing seems to come down to. Then I found this, and it suits me fine. For now.'

Her casual attitude towards changing jobs was making Vicky feel very unadventurous for staying in the same place for the last five years. For a lot more than five years in fact, since before nursing it had been school, and still in the same home area. Clarice didn't look much older than she was, either. 'How long has the Harraday Clinic been open?' she asked.

'Oh, about eighteen months, I think.' They were back in the lift now, going down to continue their inspection on the next floor. 'Simon saw a need and decided to fill it I guess, using his advantages. How did you hear about it—agency?'

'No, Si—, I mean Dr Harraday told me about it. He knows my family,' Vicky said hastily. She was annoyed with herself for nearly coming out with that betraying 'Simon' for the second time this morning, when she had planned to take care. Clarice, however, merely gave her an impish grin.

'Wish he knew mine! He's a dish, isn't he? And don't worry, we all refer to him as Simon behind his back. Half the kids do it to his face, too, because he knows their parents. He doesn't seem to mind—he's not stuffy with them.' She paused, and added thoughtfully, 'Funny really how we all refer to him as Simon and he's the boss, but Dr Asscher's always just "Dr Asscher". Not that I wouldn't rather face *him* than Simon if I'd done something wrong with a patient—that's one very steely laddie where medical practice is concerned!' She grinned, adding, 'But Dr Asscher's married with kids of his own, whereas Simon . . . well, it's almost an unfair temptation having him running around on the loose!'

'He's in the building somewhere,' Vicky said hastily, looking along the corridor into which they had just emerged.

'Yeah—went in to play with the tonsils kid, last I heard. Don't worry, the doors are thick,' Clarice said with unabated cheerfulness, though she did modify her voice a little as she began to show Vicky how everything was arranged on this floor.

It was an easily memorised pattern of small single wards, treatment rooms and sluices—thoroughly equipped, brightly-painted and cheerful. The doors had glass portholes in them so that any passing nurse could look in to check. There was a playroom which had rugs on the floor, easy chairs, and a small selection of toys. At the moment it was empty. 'For the post-op kids,' Clarice explained laconically. Vicky looked round thoughtfully, seeing the way the whole clinic had been arranged as a working hospital in miniature.

They went down some more stairs to see the pattern repeated. Medical cases on this floor, Clarice explained. A couple of other nurses passed them, one with a small child by the hand. Clarice gave Vicky a thorough tour to show her where everything was kept and then they went down the recognisable wide staircase again and were back where they started.

'That's your lot. Coffee time,' Clarice said. 'Anything I haven't told you?'

She seemed to have been pretty comprehensive. 'Pathology?' Vicky hazarded, trying to think of something she hadn't seen.

'Done by a private diagnostic unit down the road. Everything comes in from outside—laundry, disposables, and all the sterile stuff comes in from a CPU. All very centralised. We've got sterilisers for theatre, though, of course—you saw those.' Clarice darted away to pause at Sister's door and say, 'I'm in the rest room having coffee now, Sister, if you wanna buzz me!' She sounded firm about it, as if she told authority when she was going to take her coffee break rather than asking.

The rest-room was a small sitting-room, rather dark because it looked out into the road at street level and had fine net curtains across the windows. A coffee percolator was already bubbling on a table. Another nurse looked round from a mirror where she was repinning a cap on her short dark hair and introduced herself as Ruth.

Vicky looked round her with interest. At the moment, and not unnaturally, she was being moved from place to place rather like a parcel, but she supposed with a slight sense of wonder that she would soon be seeing the clinic with more familiar eyes. In fact it would soon begin to seem like home, once she had started working here. She was still contemplating the word 'home' with some doubt when Clarice said, 'If you're new to London, have you got somewhere to live yet? If you're in a hostel, don't stay there. You have to carry everything around with you, all the time, if you don't want your stuff nicked!'

'I—some friends offered to put me up.' Vicky hoped she wasn't blushing. After Clarice's earlier remarks, she could just imagine her comments if she knew the identity of the 'friends'. She really would have to look for somewhere else, whatever Simon might say about it. 'Is it difficult to find somewhere to live in London?' she asked tentatively.

'Depends what you're looking for. There's a lot of crook landlords around charging high rents and it takes time to find anywhere decent. It took Bill and me ages to find our room, and then we only got it because we knew someone who was moving out,' Clarice told her.

'There's flatsharing, of course, but you never know who you'll find yourself living with.'

The comment struck an ironic echo. 'How do I set about looking?' Vicky asked.

'Try the ads in the papers. You don't want to land yourself with two much travelling, though. Where are these friends of yours living?'

'Um—not far away. I don't actually know London at all,' Vicky said hastily, feeling rather stupid, 'so I don't really know where it is.'

'I've got an *A to Z* around somewhere.' Clarice got up from the chair she had sat down in after handing Vicky a cup of coffee and powdered milk, and wandered across to fish in a bag hanging from a set of pegs. 'What's the name of the street?'

'Er—Belville Close,' Vicky said, suddenly hoping Clarice wouldn't recognise the name. It was just as well she had taken care to notice that much this morning as they drove away from the house, because she would have felt a complete idiot not even knowing where she lived. And not knowing how to get back there either without Simon, she realised with sudden confusion.

'What's the area? What letters did it have after it?' Clarice enquired patiently when she saw Vicky's blank look.

'Oh. NW something?' Vicky said helplessly, trying to remember.

Clarice was flicking over the pages of the book in her hand and stopped to peer. 'Yeah, must be here somewhere. Belville Rise—no, that's EC10. Belville Mews . . . Belville Close. North West One. That sounds like it.' She flicked the pages again until she came up with a map. 'Hey, posh part of Camden. And really handy for getting here. I shouldn't be in a hurry to get out of there, if I were you! Can you stay?'

'Well, yes, but—'

'Then I should. Besides,' Clarice said, looking up with

a sudden wicked grin, 'you must be somewhere near the lovely Simon. He lives up that way somewhere. You never know your luck—you might run into him on a dark night!'

As a remark, it was so close to home that Vicky almost choked. She was saved from notice by the fact that Clarice's attention had turned to Ruth, who had given an amused, reproving, 'Tut tut! Honestly, Clarice!'

'Yeah, why not be honest? I'm only saying what everyone else must be thinking—anyone with normal hormones, anyway!' Clarice sounded cheerfully unrepentant. 'There's the buzzer—Paul must be awake. Off I go. There's a match this afternoon, and what do you bet that I have to haul the boyo home pie-eyed from the party afterwards? See you, Vicky. Oh, d'you want to borrow the *A to Z* until you can get one of your own? It's the best standby a girl can have—barring a reliable fella, of course!'

She shot away. Ruth, gathering herself up to move too, gave Vicky a friendly glance. 'It must be strange if you don't know London at all,' she said with a smile, 'but you'll soon find your way around, don't worry! And if you've got friends here, that'll help, won't it? Oh, and don't take any notice of Clarice. She's sex-mad, that girl. And rugger, of course!'

She left with a grin, before Vicky could try to explain that she didn't usually sit about sounding vague and helpless, it was just that everything had happened so fast. On the other hand, it wouldn't really have been easy to explain . . . Vicky sighed, and glanced at her watch, wondering what she was supposed to do next. Sister had told her she should be on duty at one and work until six. It was only half past eleven now. She wondered where Simon was, then decided that she shouldn't be wondering where Simon was, because she wasn't supposed to be depending on him, only working for him. The practical thing to do would be to go back to Sister, so she got up. The job looked promising, anyway, she told herself staunchly, and she had found Clarice likeable. And Ruth. Once she could feel more settled, she was going to enjoy herself . . . wasn't she?

Sister didn't seem surprised to see her again. In fact she handed over Vicky's navy outdoor uniform coat, saying with unruffled calm and no curiosity at all, 'Simon brought this in for you—you left it in the car. He's gone off now, but he'll be back about half past five, so you needn't worry about getting yourself home. Oh yes, he said you wouldn't have thought about lunch. There's a snack bar round the corner in Marylebone High Street which stays open on Sundays. It's a lovely morning, so I should go out and wander about a bit!'

How efficient of Simon, Vicky thought, trying to feel grateful but feeling more like a lost sheep. She would have to remember to thank him. She found herself thinking that it was just as well Clarice was going off at one and wouldn't see her getting into Simon's car. And she must find out quickly whether there was a bus which would bring her from Belville Close to here. She could just imagine the Australian girl's comments if she went on turning up in Simon's car. Besides, she'd be working at all sorts of hours, which certainly wouldn't always fit in with his. But it really was going to be difficult if she had to go on living under his roof, even if it was just as difficult to think about finding somewhere else to live.

Vicky decided to stifle her qualms and think about all that later, because it really was a lovely morning, so she slipped on her uniform coat and went cautiously out of the front door of the Harraday Clinic, grateful for Clarice's *A to Z* map book clutched in her hand. Finding her way around couldn't possibly daunt her when she had that to consult. Besides, she would soon get used to it. *All* of it.

CHAPTER FOUR

A MONTH later, Vicky could look back in wonder at how quickly she had got used to it. Used to being in London, used to the clinic's arrangement of shift hours, used to feeling that a particular child was her patient for his or her short stay. The hours were eight to one, one to six, six to eleven, and the longer night shift of eleven round to eight again, though the night shift was mainly taken on by a particular batch of nurses who had chosen night work for preference. Because of the specialling system one might find oneself working both the eight–one *and* six–eleven shifts with a long break during the afternoon, or staying on extra time if the patient's needs required it, but Vicky didn't mind that. It was odd to be working with separate single rooms instead of a large ward laid out in open-plan areas, but it very quickly began to seem second nature.

Seeing city scape all the time instead of countryside quickly became second nature too, and Vicky found that she loved London. It was so far from being all the same that at any moment one might round a corner and find a place of an entirely different character. She had found Regent's Park—such a large area of greenery that it seemed like a different world, and with a zoo in one part of it and a mosque in another, which seemed extraordinary. She had found Camden Lock and been enchanted by the suddenness of water and brightly-coloured boats right in the middle of a built-up area. It amused her to explore, and she felt light and alive as she wandered from busy traffic to quiet culs-de-sac or leapt breathlessly on and off buses. She hadn't yet tackled the Underground, not from any feeling of caution but because she liked being on the surface where she could see everything.

She wasn't quite so sure that she had got used to living with Simon. For the first few days it had been like walking on eggshells and she had jumped every time he came into a room. However, he wasn't very often in when she was, except at breakfast, when he always read the paper and communicated only in monosyllables, so that she almost got used to taking no notice of him. He was out so often in the evenings that she wondered a little if her presence drove him away. She couldn't tell whether he was also out when she was on the late shift and didn't get home until after eleven. Mostly, except at breakfast, she heard him rather than seeing him. On one rare evening when they were both in together, she had made to withdraw to her room and leave him with his sitting-room to himself, only to find him saying casually, 'You needn't be antisocial—you won't disturb me. Unless *I* disturb *you*?'

Then, of course, she had had to sit down again and try to read her book without being constantly aware of his tall figure lounging opposite her while he read *The Lancet* and, later, flicked on the television news after asking her whether she minded. That was polite of him, considering it was his house. He asked her a little later whether she was settling in all right, and if she had found the late-opening delicatessen in a nearby small street of shops he had previously told her about. His air of impersonal kindness was so different from some of their earlier confrontations that she wanted to view it with suspicion. The uneasy peace they seemed to be achieving required her to make polite answers, and she didn't like to mention that she had been looking in the evening papers for rooms to let, for fear of setting him off again with some of his taunting remarks. She had even rung a couple of numbers, but the rooms had always been taken. Vicky stayed downstairs a little longer, then

wished him a wary goodnight and escaped upstairs—
only to be stopped by his voice as she set her foot on the
first step.

'Vicky? There's no need to flinch whenever I speak to
you, you know. I may not be St George, but I'm not the
dragon, either!'

'I'm not—I mean—'

He was watching her with a lazy amusement.

'Just a thought. Oh, by the way, stick posters on your
walls if you want to make the room look more like home.
I passed by the other day when your door was open and it
looked as if you were camping. Goodnight!'

She could hardly say after that that she *was* camping,
temporarily, because it would have sounded rude. And
soon after, he had gone away for ten days to a medical
conference, leaving Dr Asscher in charge at the clinic
and Vicky to sole tenancy of the house. In fact he had
only got back last night, late, and hearing his key in the
lock had made Vicky hastily switch the television off
from the late thriller she was watching and retreat
upstairs.

She leaned her elbows on the edge of the sink, staring
absently out into the garden and thinking with a corner
of her mind that unless Simon had gone out very early,
he wasn't up yet. The children at the clinic had missed
him. Dr Asscher was a nice man, quiet, about Simon's
age but with a receding hairline already and a solemn
manner. Simon was quite a different person at work, so
much so that it provided yet another identity for him. He
showed such understanding and gentleness with the
children that even the shyest or most nervous child soon
relaxed and trusted him. He had been right when he told
her, without conceit, that he was a good doctor. Everyone missed him—only at work, of course, Vicky told
herself hastily, because of course she hadn't missed his
being here in the house, that had been a relief.

She ought to have spent her time hunting more thor-

oughly for somewhere else to live while Simon had been
out of the way, though actually she hadn't because she
had been particularly busy specialling a surgical case. An
appendix which had been grumbling for some time had
suddenly blown up so that Dr Asscher had had to make
the decision for a panicky parent. Jason had gone home
yesterday with a triumphant pride in his scar, so that was
another of her specials dealt with and gone. Simon knew
all about it because he had been on the phone from Paris
in spite of his conference. And Vicky was off duty all day
today, so she really ought to go and look at that room in
south London she'd made tentative enquiries about. It
was miles away from the clinic, though. And now that
her mother had sent up a trunk full of her things she'd
got an awful lot to move. It was a problem.

There had been a couple of phone calls at the house
for Simon while he was away. Each time a female voice
had sounded disconcerted when Vicky answered, and
neither time had the caller wanted to leave a message. It
wasn't the same voice both times, either, and Vicky
decided, as she put the phone down on the second, that
Simon obviously hadn't been wasting any time. She
hoped drily that she hadn't spoiled anything for him by
answering the calls. Still, she could hardly let it ring,
could she?

Luckily the question of exactly where Vicky was living
hadn't come up with the clinic staff. Clarice had seen
Vicky in Simon's car by now, but she had only given a
broad wink and said, 'Good on yer, that was quick
thinking!' with the obvious assumption that Vicky had
engineered the lift. And there wasn't, of course, anything to know. Nothing at all.

Vicky crushed down the memory of that kiss, which
she had pushed so firmly into the depths of her mind that
it should have sunk without trace. Her relationship with
Simon was purely a business one, and just as well too.
She paid him rent and bought her own food and tried not

to get under his feet. She ought really to go out now, just in case he was still in the house.

She didn't, though. She went on leaning dreamily on the edge of the sink and staring out of the window, feeling an odd contentment with the view. The Bursar had asked her if she wanted to sign on as a member of the clinic's permanent staff and she had agreed—after all, it was a good job. Perhaps the only disadvantage she had found was that all the clinic staff had their own busy personal lives. Clarice had her Bill, for instance, and Ruth was married, and between that and the specialling system which meant working alone rather than as part of a team, Vicky hadn't yet made a circle of friends with whom she could go out and do things. Not that it really mattered, because at home she hadn't spent much time with her fellow-nurses either. She realised abruptly, and a little guiltily, that she hadn't thought about Andrew for weeks, and not through trying not to think about him either. It was because everything else was so new, of course.

'Hallo,' Simon's voice growled behind her, and then, 'Oh, don't jump like that, you'll wake up my hangover!'

Looking at him, Vicky found herself wanting to laugh. He was leaning heavily against the doorjamb and looking very, very sorry for himself. His hair was ruffled, his dressing-gown looked as if he had dragged it on with his eyes shut and he hadn't shaved, so that the dark stubble around his jawline made him look slightly piratical, but somehow less frightening. If frightening was the right word. Vicky regarded him with the healthy amusement of a non-sufferer, and decided that she ought to take pity on him.

'Shall I make you some coffee?'

'Alka-Seltzer. It's somewhere in that cupboard. And tea, please,' he begged. He groped for the nearest chair and sat down on it while she found him the Alka-Seltzer

and ran him a glass of water to put it in. 'Ugh—never
drink brandy on an aeroplane to cure you of a hangover
you've already started to get!'

'You were celebrating?'

'Socialising. We finished the conference with a dinner.' Simon winced, and watched her while she reached
for the boiling kettle to warm the teapot. The Alka-
Seltzer, which he had drunk with a grimace, must
already be having an effect on him, since he had got as
far as opening his eyes fully, even if he was propping his
head on his hand with the martyred air of one who was
afraid it might fall off.

'Shall I make you something to eat?'

'*Eat?*'

'It might make you feel better. In fact it probably
would.'

She could hear herself sounding remarkably like Sister Mary Cadogan, which amused her. That lady's
maternal attitude must be catching. 'Think about it
while you drink your tea,' she said soothingly, and
poured it out for him, adding sugar, and putting it gently
down in front of him while she tried not to let her lips
twitch into a grin. 'You—er—do look a bit worse for
wear, I must say!'

'Hush, don't say anything, and I think I might live.'
Simon took a gulp of the tea, beginning to look as if he
might be able to laugh at himself, and then made a face.
'Yuk, why did you put sugar in it?'

'Well, you do look as if you might be in shock!'

'All right, all right! I'll drink it. Don't you dare laugh
at me.' He drank some more of the tea, and then looked
up at her with the beginning of a grin. 'Yes, I know it's
my own fault, and it's very forbearing of you not to be
telling me so!'

'Then I'll be even more forbearing and leave you in
peace, since you're obviously feeling better.' Vicky
smiled at him, and began to move. However, as she

made to pass him, one hand came out and caught at a fold of her green cotton skirt.

'No, don't go away! I seem to spend all my time seeing you vanishing out of the corner of my eye.'

'I thought you might prefer the kitchen to yourself. And I don't think you ought to try using the corners of your eyes just at the moment,' Vicky was unable to resist the retort out of a sense of mischief but she stayed where she was. 'Don't you want to read the paper? It's there.'

'No, I don't want to read the paper. The print's much too small for this morning.' He grinned at her ruefully, and pretended to wince. 'So stay here and look decorative and make me feel better! You must be off duty, since you've got your hair down.'

'Yes, I am.'

'I like it loose. All women should grow their hair long.'

'Chauvinist,' Vicky said promptly.

'No, I'm not, I'm just stating a preference. It's probably the same as most men's, but I'm still allowed to state it, aren't I?' He watched her lazily as she moved back to the window. Somehow it seemed more comfortable over there, even though the smallness of the kitchen meant she was still only three feet away from him. She poured herself out a mug of his tea as an excuse for the move, and then poured another one for Simon, because he pushed his cup hopefully in her direction. 'Have you signed on the permanent staff yet?' he enquired. 'I told the Bursar to ask you.'

'Yes, I have. Um—are you going in this morning?'

'You may well look doubtful. No, as a matter of fact I told David to stay in charge until tomorrow, in case I didn't get back. I didn't put any consultations in for today, either. Just as well,' Simon said and put up a hand to rub the back of his neck, then sighed thankfully. 'You make a good reviving pot of tea, I'm grateful to say!'

'Another thing all women should do?'

Simon gave a protesting groan. 'Don't pick a quarrel—I'm far too frail! Are you a raging feminist? If so, you should have warned me!'

'Not raging, no. Though I do believe in equality.'

'So do I. So why do I find myself in a world full of dominating females? Ah—' he put up a hand to stop her as she opened her mouth to retort, 'think twice before you come out with whatever you were going to say, and remember that equality works both ways!'

She might have told him that he was the last person to be dominated by females, quite the reverse, but she decided not to. It might bring a different note into what had been a good-humoured exchange. In fact it was surprising to realise that she had been sparring with him lightly without her usual nervousness. Perhaps it was because she was used by now to seeing him at work with the children, or perhaps it was because he was looking so far from his usual smooth self and more like an ordinary, imperfect human being. Catching the last thought, Vicky chuckled, and let him take it for an answer. He said, 'What are you doing today? Are you off all day?'

'Yes. I was specialling Jason Prince—the emergency appendix? So now I've got a day and a half off, since yesterday afternoon, in lieu of extra time.'

'Mm, I heard you were nursing him. Peter Lendell was impressed with you.' Mr Lendell was the surgeon. Vicky felt a pleased surprise that he had noticed her enough to mention it. 'I must get David to do the follow-up, and make sure he gets the fee for that one,' Simon said absently, and then, glancing up at Vicky, 'How's everything else?'

'I don't really know, I've been with Jason all the time.'

'I wasn't asking for a clinic report. I meant you. Settling in? Enjoying it? I haven't really seen you out of hours.'

He sounded quite casual and friendly, but the words seemed to bring Vicky back to employee status, reminding her of the formality with which they treated each other at work. 'Yes, thanks,' she said meekly. 'I've finished my tea so I'll just go and—'

'*Now* what have I said?' Simon gave her a mystified, slightly exasperated look. 'All right. I'll try a different tack. What are you planning on doing today?'

'Oh, I'll probably go for a walk.'

'Good, if you're not doing anything else, come down the West End with me. I've got to pick up a suit and buy a birthday present for my mother, but later we could have lunch. Okay?' He gave her a puzzled look as if he was trying to read her expression, and added with amusement, 'It's all right, I'll get dressed first! And shave! In fact I'll have a shower in a minute and put some clothes on and be ready in, oh, about three quarters of an hour. I'm feeling better already, so I'm not going to pass out on you, if that's what you're worrying about!'

'No, I wasn't. But you really don't have to take me out to lunch—'

'You don't want to? It would take up too much of your time?'

He was frowning, a blank, impersonal expression coming into his eyes, so that she was afraid she had offended him.

'I didn't mean that. I meant it's very kind of you, but you don't have to, when I'm sure you've got other things you want to do!'

'Victoria, I would like to take you out to lunch. I am not being kind, I am merely expressing a desire for your company. *Requesting* your company—is that better? Great heavens,' Simon said, amusement warring with disgust, 'you really are the most difficult girl!'

'I thought you'd probably rather I got out of your way, that's all!'

'You're not in my way, and I never ask for things I don't want. But if you don't want to come, you've only got to say so!'

'Thank you, I'd like it very much,' Vicky said quickly, knowing suddenly that she would, if he really meant it. She gave him a wary look to see if he was still offended, but he was watching her with a rueful humour in his dark eyes. 'Maybe I'd better go and change,' she said, looking down dubiously at her blouse and skirt. 'I was only going to look round a few shops and see if there were any clothes I wanted to buy.'

'You look fine as you are. And there are plenty of shops to look round.' Simon grinned at her, casually good-humoured now if still with a touch of puzzlement in his eyes. 'You really should stop avoiding me—house-mate!—or I'll start to wonder if I've grown two heads! And one's enough,' he added, 'to have the tail-end of a hangover in. But I promise I'll be fully recovered by the time we go out, all right?'

She had assumed that they would part to shop and meet up again at some pre-arranged place for lunch, but Simon seemed to have other ideas. As they set off in the car he said, 'Think of something I can buy for my mother, which I can send through the post. My mind's gone blank!'

'Scarf? Handkerchief? A book?'

'I'm not sure what she reads. A scarf might do. You can help me choose one.'

'How can I, when I wouldn't have the least idea what she'd like?'

'Oh, anything of impeccably good taste. We'll choose it by the label, shall we?' He sounded amused. 'A scarf should be nice and light to send abroad, anyway, it'll go in an envelope. She won't live in England, she says it's grubby.'

'What, *all* of it?'

Simon chuckled, but didn't answer because he was negotiating a way round a parked delivery van. A moment later he said, 'We'll park in an underground car-park I know of, and then walk through to Bond

Street, if that's all right with you. If you're on a clothes hunt, we can go all round Fenwicks. Now I wonder . . . do I need a shirt?'

'A suit, you said?'

'Yes, I must pick that up later. The medical profession stays formal,' he said idly, 'so one must dress as expected. Anything else in particular you've got to get?'

'Tights,' Vicky said meekly. It was extraordinarily domestic to be discussing their joint shopping and felt quite unreal.

'Okay, that's easy. And when you wear your uniform dress,' he said mischievously, 'I can be chauvinistically glad to see you in black ones!'

She had to pull a face at him for that, and resolve to wear overalls and ordinary-coloured tights for at least the next few times she was on duty. Lately she'd been alternating between her own blue uniform and clinic whites, and nobody seemed to mind which she wore. Or perhaps she'd start going in for Dior tights in bright pastel colours, as Clarice did now and again, and see what Simon made of that. Remembering his easy but totally professional manner at work she was suddenly aware of him as Dr Harraday of the Harraday Clinic, her boss, and it froze her back into shyness for a moment. He wasn't, by any stretch of the imagination, just an ordinary acquaintance—and it was going to be difficult trying to behave as if he was, and as if it wasn't very odd to be going shopping as well as lunching with him.

It turned out not to be difficult at all, because Simon was amazingly cheerful company. She found herself relaxing with him and arguing amicably over what she wanted or didn't want, and whether London would be colder than the country when winter came. They chose a scarf for his mother, in silk with a delicate spray of deep pink flowers on it. Vicky picked it out because it seemed the closest to 'impeccable taste' and, besides, she thought it was pretty. Simon agreed and bought it, though the price turned out to be something Vicky considered outrageous.

She bought her tights while he was looking at shirts, and stuffed them quickly in her bag before he could see what colour they were. He didn't seem to mind that she wanted to wander round all the departments at Fenwicks, which was remarkably good-humoured of him, and apart from his tendency to point out clothes which she had already walked past knowing they wouldn't suit her, he was quite useful at guiding her round the store. Some girlfriend or other must have lugged him out shopping in the past, Vicky decided, and on fairly frequent occasions too, because he seemed knowledgeable about female attire, and where to find what bits of it. However, it seemed to amuse him to walk round with Vicky and offer unwanted advice.

She didn't buy anything, though she looked quite hard at a striped woollen skirt, thinking that she might come back another time and try that on when Simon wasn't with her. Eventually they had finished their tour and it seemed to be time for lunch. It was no use asking her where she wanted to go, she told Simon, because she hadn't the least clue. They were outside in the street again by now and wandering idly.

'We-ell . . . I know, there's a new place round the corner which I noticed a couple of weeks ago. Let's try that, shall we?'

Vicky hoped it wouldn't be too smart, with a sudden return of self-consciousness. It wasn't—the waiters were in jeans. The decor was of the stripped pine variety with scarlet awnings to make it look as if the whole thing had been transplanted from a holiday resort—or from a Cinzano commercial, Simon suggested drily, making her giggle. It was fairly full, but they found a table and sat down next to each other on a scarlet-upholstered bench against the wall. Simon, pretending to wince, said that he wasn't quite sure he could take all that much bright colour after this morning and Vicky looked at him with a grin.

'You can't have been *that* bad, because when you went to dress I heard you whistling in the shower.' She glanced up, suddenly aware that a waiter was standing beside them, and wanted to blush.

Simon, however, didn't seem to notice anything unusual because he made matters worse by saying, 'Yes, but you'd cured me with tea and sympathy by then. Living with a nurse has definite advantages. What's the chef's special, I wonder?'

The waiter told him, and then proved he'd heard the rest of the conversation by asking if they wanted wine, or would sir rather stick to tomato juice? The 'sir' was said with a comic intonation rather than a formal one, and the waiter didn't look in the least curious about whether they were living together or not. Vicky tried to let her embarrassment subside and concentrate on choosing something from the mainly Italian menu. They both decided they didn't want to drink and the waiter went away with their order. Vicky wondered for a moment whether to raise the subject of her attempts to search for somewhere else to live, but it seemed a pity to spoil the relaxed mood and, anyway, Simon had started telling her about the Barbican Centre in the City which had come up in conversation between them earlier.

'I'll take you there some time if you like. Do you want to go to a concert, or a play? I know one or two actors with the RSC, so—Oh, excuse me a minute, will you? There's someone over there I want to see.'

The 'someone' was a girl who was just leaving. Vicky could understand why anyone would want to see her, because she was quite incredible to look at. She had blue-black hair in an aureole round her head and one of those perfect, Eurasian faces with an apricot skin and wide slanting eyes. She was quite stunningly beautiful, and she was also very tall and slim with the fine-boned thinness of a top photographic model—in fact Vicky was sure she had seen her in several fashion magazines. She was wearing a combination of burnt-orange and cerise which, on her, somehow didn't clash but merely looked exotic. She greeted Simon with a cry of delight and kissed him on both cheeks. They exchanged a few sentences, and then she kissed him again and departed with a wave. Vicky looked down at the food the waiter had just put in front of her and wondered why she suddenly didn't feel hungry.

'That was Jazalee,' Simon said explanatorily, sliding into place beside her, 'a friend of my sister's. Sorry, but I had a message for her. Oh good, this veal looks as if they can cook tolerably, doesn't it?'

'A friend of my sister's' sounded suspiciously like an excuse. 'You have a sister?' Vicky asked politely, mainly because she felt she ought to say something.

'Not *a* sister—several. Far too many. None of them around at the moment, I'm glad to say. Like that American diplomat, they have an infinite capacity for taking planes.' Simon was eating placidly and with good appetite, and she felt him glance at her. 'Jazalee was at school with one of them, I forget which.'

'Do you have brothers too?'

'No. The family does seem to run overwhelmingly to girls,' Simon said gloomily, but with a note in his voice which made Vicky suspect he was actually quite fond of his sisters. 'They're called Mel, Steph, Cat, and Liz, in descending order, if you'd care to know. That *is* four, isn't it? Yes, I thought it was. Don't let's discuss my sisters, who have a tendency to try to take over my life if I'd let them. What were we talking about?'

'I can't remember,' Vicky said, though she could. It had been very kind of Simon to begin an offer to take her out, but there was no need to remind him of it and make him feel he had to complete it. She found herself trying to visualise Simon with four sisters, no doubt all of them with the same sort of striking looks as himself. Marina must have fitted in well amongst that kind of circle. Vicky crushed the thought down, and the subsequent idea that he could find consolation amongst his sister's friends, though doubtless he could find his own consolation without any difficulty. She took a mouthful of her lunch, and heard Simon say amiably,

'Were we still talking about clothes? Why wouldn't you try on those dungarees, by the way? The grey cord ones with the contrasting leg-warmers? They would have suited you!'

'No they wouldn't!' Jazalee had been wearing dungarees, orange silk ones. Vicky went on quickly to cover the snap in her voice, 'You have to be tall to wear trousers—well, except for ordinary jeans for doing the housework in!'

'Nonsense. You just have not to be fat. And you're not. I'm only trying to cure you of going round looking so prim and proper,' Simon said outrageously, with a teasing note in his voice. He blinked as he met Vicky's glare.

'I am *not* prim and proper! I'm just small, and I can hardly help that, can I?'

'Why should you want to help it? Small is beautiful. That's a well-known phrase.'

'Oh don't—don't tease,' Vicky said crossly. She was aware that she was behaving badly when he had been kind enough to take her out to lunch, let alone escorting her round the shops which must have been a great waste of his time. She opened her mouth to say something more, perhaps an apology, but Simon got in first.

'Good heavens, I believe you really do mind. There's nothing wrong with being small, little one. In fact I should have thought it had great advantages!'

The 'little one' didn't help. Neither did the kind note in his voice. 'Well I couldn't exactly go round dressing like what's-her-name, and expecting it to suit me, could I?' Vicky pointed out, feeling ruffled.

'Not many people could look like Jazalee. You'd need to have a Persian mother and a Russian-Chinese father, for starters. She really is amazingly beautiful, isn't she?' Simon said tranquilly. 'Sweet-natured, too. She's just got herself engaged to a French photographer, and he's about the size of a gnome, I believe! Are you going to eat your lunch, or don't you like it?'

'Oh, yes, it's—it's very nice. Thank you.' Vicky took another mouthful, feeling foolish. After a moment she glanced at him defensively. 'There aren't any particular advantages in being small, as a matter of fact, but I haven't got a complex about it! Just in case that's what you were thinking!'

'Oh dear me no. I just thought you were a very militant female. With eyes which flash green fire,' Simon said with a caressing note in his voice, but a mocking glint in his eyes. 'You can't expect any sympathy from me, when I've just spent ten days sleeping with my feet over the end of a standard-sized hotel bed! There now, you hadn't thought of that, had you? That's the other side of the coin, and the disadvantage of being six foot three!'

She had to laugh at that, and over coffee a few minutes later he started to chat about different parts of London, so that Vicky could join in and tell him which bits she knew and which she didn't. It reminded her all over again about the room she ought to go and see and she also couldn't help remembering that, to her knowledge, Simon hadn't had a whole day off since she started work for him. As he paid the bill and they wandered outside she was thinking that there must be things he wanted to do besides escorting one ordinary girl about, so she had better make sure he didn't feel he had to take her home again. As he paused on the pavement she said quickly,

'Thank you very much for the lunch. Don't forget to

pick up your suit, but you don't have to look after me any more, because I—I've got to go and look at a room in Clapham I might rent!'

'You've *what*?' He looked as startled as if she'd said she was going to the moon. 'What's wrong with where you're living now? And if there's something wrong, why haven't you said so?'

'Oh n—no, there isn't anything, it's just that I'm sure you'd be quite glad to get rid of me!'

'If I wanted to get rid of you I'd have said so.' He was looming over her, making her feel self-consciously that passers-by would see his annoyance. 'What *is* all this? I thought we were getting on perfectly well! Have you picked up a boyfriend you're planning to move in with? Because if so, I'm going to take a look at him before I let you do anything so idiotic!'

'No, I certainly haven't, and it isn't anything like that! And don't be so—so bossy!' Vicky told him, outraged out of any shyness. 'I'm not one of your sisters!'

'No, you're not, are you? Nearly—but not quite.' Simon said the words with a dangerous edge. It reminded Vicky abruptly that he might have been her brother-in-law, if . . . 'So you want to dissolve our mutual protection society, do you?' Simon said, with an undertone of sarcasm which struck Vicky as unnecessarily nasty. 'Are you still striking your Victorian attitudes, by any chance? And if so, shall I remind you that wherever you run off to live, you may find yourself sharing a house with men? Terrify you though that may, it's quite likely to happen! And as for going right off to South London where you'll have to travel through goodness knows what in the middle of the night, that's plain ridiculous. Good God, do you dislike me that much?'

'No, of course I don't! Do we have to quarrel in the street?' Vicky hissed, caught between anger and self-consciousness. 'And I am *not* terrified of men!'

'You could have fooled me. I seem to remember

saying that to you once before,' Simon drawled odiously. 'And the street's where we happen to be. London really is no place for an innocent out on the loose.'

'I'm not a child,' Vicky said in a dangerously quiet voice.

'No, you're not, and you don't behave like an idiot at work, either. You look remarkably like a child standing there glowering at me, though!' His lips twitched on an involuntary laugh, and she could see him lapsing into one of his rapid changes of mood. 'Oh, come on, Vicky! Do stop being so prickly! Make up?'

He had reached for her hand, and was giving her such a winning smile that she wanted to smile back at him. And in the end, unwillingly, she did. She wished, with a despairing corner of her mind, that he couldn't turn on the charm so effectively. It was unfair. He had a completely false picture of her, and threw it at her at the least opportunity.

'All right,' she said in a small dignified voice.

'And you won't dissolve our mutual protection society?'

'All right,' she said again, but added, with a touch of tartness, 'though I don't know why you have to call it that! I can't see *you* being in need of protection!'

'Little do you know. They're coming at me from all sides. Maybe I just like having somebody around who actually does the washing up,' Simon told her, on a mocking note. 'You do have your uses!'

'Thank you. But you don't have to go on entertaining me, in exchange, when I'm sure you've got people you'd rather see! And you don't have to take me home, either! No, it's all right, I won't go to Clapham!' she added hastily, as he began to frown, 'I—I think I'll go and have my hair cut!'

She had forgotten his earlier remarks, but he obviously hadn't, because he made an exasperated sound. 'Oh no! Just because of what I said? All right, all right—

it's your hair, you wretched girl! But I'll tell you one thing—if you must have it cut, you'll have it done properly! And I shall take you to the right place now! Don't argue, because I'm not in the mood for any more arguments!'

Towed along against her stifled protest, Vicky knew that she should have remembered he was impulsive and believed in getting his own way. The quiet, gentle side of her nature seemed to disappear completely when she was with Simon, and leave her instinctively fighting for survival.

He halted abruptly in front of an emporium which had all the hallmarks of a top salon, and swept her inside before she could object that it was definitely the sort of place one couldn't get into without an appointment so it wasn't somewhere she could have her hair done now. Inside, Simon dumped her in a chair with a threatening, 'Don't move!', exchanged a cheerful word with a blonde receptionist who seemed to know him suspiciously well, and disappeared into some inner region. Vicky looked round cautiously, seeing the jewellery glinting in display cases, the padded cream walls and the signed photographs of famous faces, among them several well-known actresses. The whole place looked very expensive—but Vicky consoled her quaking nerves with the thought that she'd just been paid. She hadn't been given time to notice what the place was called, but she suspected it was one of those places everybody had heard of—and Simon had walked in as if he felt perfectly at home there. She was still contemplating that fact when he reappeared, just as she was feeling tempted to beat a retreat.

'It's all right, Leon will do you himself, and I've persuaded him to fit you in,' he said, wearing the tail-end of a smile which seemed to belong to some highly satisfactory conversation he'd just been having. Vicky decided that he'd probably come across several girls he knew being beautified, and had paused to flirt with all of them—but as she opened her mouth to say something a junior appeared to usher her into the inner salon.

'I'll be back to pick you up,' Simon said clearly and firmly, giving Vicky the feeling that she wasn't to be let out until he reappeared. And then he was gone.

A very long time later, Vicky stared at herself in the mirror with disbelieving wonder. That was her?

A curly, shining mane of hair framed her face in a mass of gleaming light brown, even the colour looking warmer, a dark honey. It fell as naturally as if she were lucky enough to have hair which simply grew that way. Leon, who was plainly the salon's owner and right at the top of his profession from the way everybody treated him, had decided she was to keep it long, but layered into lightness and permed into soft waves and curls. He hadn't actually altered the colour, merely worked magic with scissors and shampoos and conditioners.

He was almost as smooth as Simon, and Vicky had started out by being terrified of him, but ended up responding to his charm so that he seemed almost like a friend. He had inspected her from all angles before he decided to do anything at all, had lifted her hair and shaken it about with what appeared to be approval, and had made complimentary remarks about her cheek-bones. Then he had sent her away to be washed, had her brought back and set about her expertly with scissors, sent her away again for a light perm . . . She had managed to tell him, shyly, that if she didn't have her hair short it must be possible to put it up under a nurse's cap, but he had demonstrated how easy that would be by piling it up with an expert flick of his fingers. Now, he stood beside her being charmingly friendly, and telling her to toss her head to see how beautifully the style fell back into place. If she wanted to wash it herself, he said, she could shake it dry while running her fingers through it, because the perm would hold the curls in spite of the length. Vicky, staring at herself, felt like Cinderella.

Leon had said it would be a style to suit her and one plainly didn't argue with his judgment. He had been right, if that was really herself, because she looked quite . . . different. Even her eyes looked a different shape, larger and tilted a little at the corners, while her face against the mass of hair looked appealingly small, thinner, more sculptured. She really *had* got cheekbones. She was still gazing at herself after the first disbelieving gulp when Leon had finally turned her round towards the mirror, and trying to concentrate on his instructions, when he glanced round and said, 'Oh, hallo, Simon. That was good timing, we've just finished. It looks marvellous, doesn't it?'

'Mm. Oh yes, I like that.' Simon's face appeared behind her head in the mirror, and his eyes studied her with approval. 'Definitely,' he drawled.

'Not, of course, that I'd have followed those strict orders of yours if I hadn't agreed,' Leon said, sounding amused. 'Well, Vicky? You haven't said anything. Like it?'

'Oh yes! It's lovely! I mean—'

'There you are, Leon, you've stunned her into silence. And that, I may tell you, is unusual,' Simon said on a laugh. 'Come on then, beautiful—since you're ready, I can stop parking on a double yellow line and risking a parking ticket!'

'Don't let him bully you,' Leon advised, 'and if he gets a ticket it's his own fault. It's on the account, isn't it, Simon?' He must have said that because he saw Vicky fumbling with her bag, and he was turning away before she could say anything else. 'See you again some time— bye now!'

One didn't tip a top salon owner, that much she did know. Vicky murmured a hasty goodbye in the direction of his retreating back, knowing that she ought to have said something more to him but feeling as if her tongue had frozen, and followed Simon obediently out of the salon. Her head felt light and she kept being aware of soft curls whipping against her cheek. She was also wondering, in a dazed fashion, how many girls had their hair paid for by Simon, if he had an account here. She got into the Porsche and they had roared away before she finally found her voice.

'Thank you, but you shouldn't.'

'Not at all. Put it down to being bossy. That was what you called me, wasn't it?' Simon sounded amused and pleased with himself. 'Don't you dare start offering to pay me back, either!'

'What did he mean about your "strict orders"?'

'Yes, I was afraid you'd have picked that up. I told him not to cut it short, even if you wanted it that way.' Simon cast her a slanting, triumphant, lightly mocking glance before returning his eyes to the road. 'I reckon even you wouldn't dare to destroy a Leon haircut, though, on a principle!'

'I wouldn't want to.' If he was expecting her to be cross, she couldn't be. She felt light-hearted as well as light-headed, so that she wanted to bubble into laughter over his stubbornness and arrogance instead of thinking about anything else at all. 'Thank you for taking me there,' she said meekly, but unable to keep the humour out of her voice.

'You're welcome. I'm glad you won't go and have your head shaved, just to annoy me!'

'Oh, much too difficult for a nurse's cap! And besides, it might frighten the children.' She was tempted to add that if shaven heads were in fashion, she was sure Simon would know of a tattooist to drag her off to for decoration—but they were already swooping round the corner into Belville Close and drawing up outside the house. She turned her head to smile at him and saw that he was looking at her with an odd intentness.

'Mm. I really do approve. And I'm even more sure

that you shouldn't be let out on the loose! You might get kidnapped.'

'By mistake, or on purpose?' Vicky asked, laughing, and scrambled out of the car before he could answer. A light breeze whipped her curls round her face and she brushed them back, shaking her head to feel the unfamiliar lightness all over again. Cinderella, with Simon as an unlikely fairy godmother, she thought with a giggle. All she needed now was a glass slipper. She went ahead of him to open the front door because he was collecting some packages out of the back of the car, and she had reached the stairs by the time he caught up with her.

'Here. I bought you something.' He put a large wrapped parcel into her hand as she paused. It felt soft through the wrappings, like some kind of material, and she looked up at him in surprise.

'Why? What is it?'

'You'll have to take it upstairs and see, since you can't very well try it on down here!'

She had already started upstairs obediently before his words got through to her, and she stopped abruptly, swinging round to look at him. 'But you can't—'

'It's no use telling someone they can't do something when they already have,' Simon told her, with a glint of challenge in his eyes.

'But you can't—' she began again, and then stopped. Because she was above him on the stairs they were suddenly on the same level, and he was very close to her. She was abruptly aware of the warm dark brown of those mocking eyes, so near that she could almost have counted the lighter hazel flecks in them, and of the texture of his skin, and of the cool curve of his mouth. She felt dizzy suddenly—but perhaps that was because his eyes had lost their mockery and had that intent look in them again.

'Definitely on purpose,' he murmured, mystifyingly,

and leaned forward to kiss her lightly on the lips. Then there was a light thud as he dropped whatever he was holding, and his arms came round her, holding her against him, his lips seeking hers with a sudden urgency. Vicky swayed against him, feeling the hard demand of his mouth on hers, the shivers of sweetness which fragmented all over her body, the close, warm, maleness of him . . .

The telephone began to ring somewhere above them.

Simon let her go. 'Saved by the bell,' he murmured sardonically, 'and just when I was proving that you do look good enough to eat.' He lifted her lightly out of his way, and went past her up the remaining stairs with his long stride.

Vicky stayed where she was until she suddenly remembered where she was, and that she ought not to be. She was still holding the package Simon had given her, and she stooped automatically to pick up the one he had dropped—his suit, presumably—before she walked decorously up the rest of the stairs. Kissing was something Simon took lightly, and was just another part of the teasing, challenging game he chose to play with her—except at work of course, where they were both quite different. She reached the sitting-room door to find him coming towards her, but he was wearing his impersonal, busy look, and when she held his dropped package out towards him he merely glanced at it, and at her.

'Put it on my bed, there's a good girl. That was my answering service, and I've got to go out again. See you later, probably!'

He went past her, and a moment later the front door slammed behind him. Vicky stood still, trying not to feel resentment at the way he could pick her up and drop her as easily as his parcel, and for as little reason. She reminded herself firmly that he was a doctor, and his answering service certainly had to take precedence over everything else—if, of course, the message had been about a patient. So she had better go and put his suit on his bed like the good girl he had called her and then see what sort of present he had, bossily and with casual generosity, bought her.

Several moments later, up in her room, Vicky was regarding the contents of her package, which she had laid out carefully and with disbelief on her bed. A very beautiful, cream-coloured, crepe de Chine blouse, with a ruffled neck, and a wide frill running right down the front. A stunning evening waistcoat in black satiny material, embroidered all round the edges with a pattern of coloured sequins. And a pair of black trousers in the same satin, expertly cut and pleated at the waist into a high cummerbund.

He had even got her size exactly right, though she seemed to remember that that had come up, sometime, during their tour round the shops.

They were certainly the most fashionable clothes Vicky had ever had, and even if they had been bought to prove a point, she knew she ought to be grateful. Instead she found herself feeling resentful and remembering that Marina had always been a trendy dresser. Fairy godfather was out to transform her with a vengeance, it seemed. She wondered with a touch of annoyance, when on earth Simon expected her to wear this outfit. It really was beautiful, though it probably wouldn't suit her.

Since he was safely out of the house, she tried it on. Somehow with the hairstyle it really did suit her—it was quite amazing. She looked even more like someone else. Someone quite, quite different from the Vicky she was used to.

She remembered very suddenly that he had called her his 'mutual protection'. As such, perhaps he had to turn her into someone else. Someone who would look more like a girl he might be expected to be living with. She tore the clothes off quickly and flung them on the bed, then picked them up carefully and hung them in her wardrobe. No, she wasn't going to give them back to him. She wasn't going to look as if she minded. In fact, she would thank him, very sweetly, very lightly—and make sure that she never, ever, took anything he did or said seriously.

CHAPTER FIVE

'WE'VE been invited to a party.'

'*We* have?' Vicky asked, on a querying note.

'Well, it's addressed to Number 10, and that's both of us, isn't it?' Simon passed the envelope across the breakfast table.

It had obviously been delivered by hand. The invitation sticking out of it was signed 'Chris and Terry' and the date was a week ahead. Chris—she was the blonde from opposite, with whom Vicky had exchanged smiles by now, though no more than that because both of them always seemed to be passing each other in a hurry. Terry, by elimination, must be the bearded man who also seemed to live there, and who might be Chris's husband. Or something. Vicky looked dubiously at the invitation, and said, 'But they don't know *me* . . .'

'Well, they will by the time you've gone to their party, won't they? I wonder what this one's for—does it say?'

'No. It just says, "Dress up, we're celebrating", with three exclamation marks.'

'Oh? Oh, I know—Chris's new job. They've just made her an editor. Television,' Simon added explanatorily, being unusually talkative for breakfast time. 'What was she before? Researcher? Vision mixer? I can't remember. I don't watch enough to notice the names that come up on the credits, but I'd better not say that when we go, had I? Good, with a week's notice you can fix your shifts with Sister, and I know I haven't got anything on that night. Are you almost ready? I've got to go in early today, so I'll give you a lift.'

'Thanks,' Vicky said meekly. He seemed to take it for granted that she would go to this party with him, but since she suddenly found she rather wanted to go, it didn't seem worth while arguing over it. It would be a good chance, she thought, to wear those clothes which had been hanging in her wardrobe for the past ten days. After all, the invitation did say 'Dress up'. And besides, it would be a change to meet some non-medical people.

She got up from the breakfast table and did her usual quick clearing away. If Simon was going in unusually early that would make her early for her eight a.m. shift, but she could only be grateful he was since it was drizzling outside. 'Are you coming into the clinic?' she asked over her shoulder, wondering who they'd got who was ill enough for him to want to see first thing in the morning.

'No, but I'll drop you there. I'm going in to my rooms. There's someone I want to phone at Bart's before he starts his operating list, and I know he's starting at eight forty-five.' Simon stretched as he got up, avoiding Vicky neatly as she dodged round him. He really did look remarkably good-tempered this morning, she decided, and found herself wondering drily whether he'd had a good evening the night before. He'd been out somewhere, she knew. Perhaps she should refuse to go to the party with him so that he could take whoever it was who'd caused this lingering cheerfulness. She squashed the thought quickly. She'd been invited, and besides, if he'd asked for a 'mutual protection society', he'd get one.

It was funny, she thought with a touch of wistfulness, how well they'd been getting on since that row about her moving out. It was almost as if her changed hairstyle had given her the confidence to deal with him—though surely it couldn't have made her *that* different!

'Who've you got today?' he asked as he followed her down the stairs.

'Charly,' she reminded him. The Honourable Charlotte Ryder, aged fourteen, was recovering from pneumonia, which she had developed mainly as a result of taking a patent cold-cure so that she could go out disco dancing and then coming back late at night without a coat. Vicky hesitated for a moment, thinking about her patient, and then added thoughtfully, 'Will you be in later today?'

'Worried? About Charly?'

'Not the pneumonia, she's responding all right to the antibiotics. I wondered if you knew what her appetite's usually like? I'm probably fussing, but—'

'The thinness? I'm not her GP, unfortunately—she's a referral. Anorexic, you think?'

'Not yet, but I wondered if she could be heading that way.' There was a pause while they both made a quick dash through the rain to the car. Once safely inside, Vicky said breathlessly, apologetically, 'You'd probably already thought of it.'

'What with it being so fashionable and all. Yes, I'd noticed. She's not likely to feel much like eating at the moment, but it needs watching. See what you can notice about her attitude, and I'll come in and talk to you about it later. If she is going in that direction, it'd be as well to catch her early.' Simon sighed. 'Difficult one to treat. Even more difficult without co-operation, and I'm not sure we'd get it from that particular GP. I don't know about the family. Oh well. Did you nurse any anorexics where you were before?'

'Yes, a couple, but we were in such specialised departments they tended to move them to psychiatric. One just looks out for it, nowadays. Just as one looks out for unexplained bruises,' Vicky added wryly, remembering the other far too common reason for children to be admitted to hospital.

'Children at risk? Yes. We've had one or two of those, as well. Oh, it happens in all walks of life,' Simon said to Vicky's look of surprise, 'surely you know that, with all your training?'

'Theoretically. But somehow—'

'You don't expect it among the privileged? It's there, all the same.' Simon drew up outside the clinic. The streets, moderately empty so early in the morning, had brought them there rapidly. 'Hard to be understanding rather than angry, yes, I know. But one has to be. Hop out—I'll see you later.'

Scuttling in to the clinic out of the rain as he roared away, Vicky reflected that working here wasn't really all that different from her hospital experience. In fact if she looked back at the short-stay illnesses which had brought children into her ward at Pensbury the pattern was remarkably similar—gastro-enteritis, pneumonia, broken bones, chest infections, ear infections, appendix, tonsils. Abdominal pains, in for investigation. Diabetics, asthmatics. It was only the more serious long-stay cases which were missing from the clinic—the infant cancers and leukaemias, severe rheumatology cases, young cardiac cases coming in for valve operations or other heart surgery—and those had little to do with money or the lack of it. As she thought about it, her mind went at once to the one serious, long-term case she had met in the clinic—Sebastian, the ten-year-old boy who came in to use the dialysis machine. Somehow, almost the most heart-wrenching thing about Sebastian wasn't his smallness and paleness and invariable good behaviour. It wasn't Sebastian himself at all, but the fact that his twin brother Ben always came with him. Ben, cheerful, practical, bright-eyed and healthy, was the exact image of the way Sebastian ought to be, and to see him settling down across the room from his brother, to hear the light young voice say, 'Shall I read, then, Twin?' had brought Vicky nearer to tears than almost anything else in her nursing career.

'You're in nice and early! Hey, what's the matter— lost a pound and found fifty pence?'

'Sorry!' Vicky came out of her thoughts rapidly to

greet the night nurse who had spoken to her—one she knew, who had recently changed over from days, having decided that permanent night-work would suit her better. 'I was thinking about the twins,' she admitted, a little shamefacedly.

'Bas and Ben? I don't see them now. He's not worse, is he?' At Vicky's shake of the head, the girl touched her arm understandingly. 'Yes, I know, it got me too when I first knew them. Still does, sometimes. Here's hoping they find Bas a compatible kidney soon. It's a shame he's got such a difficult blood group, isn't it? Oh, by the way, your little madam had a better night last night!'

'Charly? Better-behaved, or sleeping better?'

'Both,' the other girl said with a grin. 'But you're still welcome to her. She's a spoiled brat, that one. I should think you'll be glad when she goes home. Look, since you're so early, have yourself some coffee before you go up and get the night report on her—there's still some in the pot.'

Vicky had been a little surprised to find the night staff invariably referring to Charly as 'the little madam', since she didn't find her so difficult herself. She wouldn't, either, have thought Charly was spoiled. As she hung up her coat and pinned on a paper cap, she wondered thoughtfully why Charly always did behave worse at nights—for attention? Could she be afraid of the dark? If she was on the edge of anorexia there could be a clue to it there, because it was an illness which could come from a desire not to grow up, a longing to return to the undeveloped state of childhood. That might seem an odd thing to decide about Charly who, after all, was in here as a result of being determined to go out dancing half the night—but adolescence was such a mixed state that it was still possible. A desperate longing for security, combined with a rebellion against security, was one of the characteristics of the teenage years.

Perhaps she was worrying unduly, because Charly

accepted her breakfast with better grace than usual and
Vicky, staying in the room with her on the excuse of
checking through her notes, was able to see that she did
actually eat some of it. Her temperature was down and
she was looking rested, so it seemed fair to give in to her
pleading to use the telephone later because she 'simply
must ring Camilla because she hadn't talked to her for
ages'. It was still school holidays, so Camilla would
apparently be at home with nothing to do, particularly
since Charly wasn't there to amuse her. Catching the
beginning of the conversation after she had brought in
the telephone trolley, Vicky was amused to notice that
Charly was assuming a certain self-importance about
managing to get pneumonia in the summer! If that was
going to be the new status symbol, Vicky thought wryly,
at least it was better than some—it was easier to treat!

She let Charly have quarter of an hour before she went
back, filling in the time by helping to change the bed-
linen around Luke who, at twelve, should have known
better than to manage to break both legs while pretending to be a Harrier Jump Jet. He seemed more upset by
the fact that he'd broken his new watch at the same time,
and a glance at his notes suggested to Vicky that he was
accident prone. He'd already managed to fall through a
greenhouse roof, knock himself out playing football,
and get concussed falling out of a tree. His parents were
apparently devoted to him if slightly despairing about his
sense of adventure. He was cheerful and chunky with a
gap-toothed grin and bright red hair, and it was impossible not to laugh at his ability to pull truly dreadful faces.

Going back down to the medical floor to her own
patient, Vicky couldn't help contrasting Luke's round
face with Charly's bony one—surely the child *was* a little
too thin, even given a difference in bone structure and
the fact that Charly had just had pneumonia? Trying to
pin down the exact cause of her unease, Vicky decided
that it wasn't the young girl's slightness, because she was

small-boned and might be a thin type anyway. It was Charly's face which bothered her. There was something about the way the skin drew back tightly away from her nose and across her cheekbones, giving her a much older look than she should have had and reducing her natural prettiness.

She found Charly bright-eyed and flushed and wondered guiltily if she had let her talk too long, but it seemed to be due to moodiness, not a sudden rise in temperature, and she had already finished her call. Vicky moved quietly and calmly, ignoring the sulky looks Charly was darting at her as she put the trolley outside the door in case anyone else wanted it, picked up a couple of magazines which had slipped to the floor, checked Charly's pulse, and poured her out a drink which the girl promptly shrugged away. Vicky gave her a thoughtful look, and said cheerfully, 'You can have a bath this morning. In fact you can have it now. I've just looked, and Greville's finished having his, so the bathroom's free!'

'Ugh, I'm not sure if I want to have a bath after him, he's disgusting!'

'What, because he was sick in the night? He can't help having digestive problems—that's what he's in here for!'

'Because he's so *fat*! I bet his mother brings him extra food all the time! She's just that type.'

Privately Vicky agreed with her. She knew that Greville's mother, a very possessive and over-protective lady, had had to be dissuaded from bringing him extra snacks from home which would have totally spoiled his careful controlled diet. It was true too that the boy in the next room was grossly overweight—though that hardly excused the spiteful revulsion in Charly's voice.

'No, his mother isn't allowed to bring him extra food,' she said calmly. 'I think she'd like to because she loves him, and it's a sort of maternal instinct to feed one's young, isn't it? Haven't you ever seen a mother bird with a nestful of chicks? Now, about that bath—you did say you were sick of being sponged down in bed, so I thought you'd be delighted to be let out to the bathroom at last!'

'Oh, I don't care—'

Abruptly and without warning, Charly burst into tears. Vicky moved quickly, instinctively, to put her arms round her, reaching her before the child could pull away and holding her with gentle firmness. She couldn't help noticing that Charly turned into her arms like a small child after only the barest struggle, sobs shaking her slight form in wordless spasms. 'Hey,' Vicky said gently, 'that's a lot of fuss to make about a bath. What's the matter, honey? Did you quarrel with your friend on the phone?'

'N—no . . .'

'Well, what, then?' Vicky asked calmly, as the muffled voice said no more. Charly had her face buried against her shoulder and didn't make any protest as Vicky stroked the soft fair hair with one comforting hand.

'N—nothing . . . I'm all right.' The sobs were lessening into an occasional hiccup. 'I j—just want to go home—'

The words, oddly, sounded scared. 'Well, you will, soon,' Vicky pointed out. 'You're almost better, aren't you? Mm? But there's no point in sending you out until you are better. You'd only sit around at home feeling too tired to do anything. I tell you what, though, when Dr Harraday comes in we'll ask him when he thinks you'll be fit to go. Okay?'

Charly was pulling out of her arms now, and Vicky let her go, standing quite still where she was beside the bed as the young girl scrabbled in a Kleenex box for a tissue, and blew her nose fiercely. She didn't look at Vicky directly, and was plainly searching for dignity. 'You d—don't have to tell him I was crying, do you?' she asked defensively.

'Not unless it's important.' It was a way of putting it which avoided the lie. 'Okay now?'

'Yes, I'm fine. I—I think I will have that bath—can I?'

'Sure. I'll go and run it for you.'

'I can wash my face before I go out of here, can't I?'

'You don't even have to ask,' Vicky said with a smile, and reached behind the locker for Charly's spongebag. 'But I'll bring you a wet flannel over from the basin if you like, so that you don't even have to get out of bed. Right? Now, I'll go and run that bath and then I'll come back for you. You might feel a bit wobbly walking about today, since you've only been up for bedmaking so far. Back in a minute or two!'

She was still wondering exactly what had set Charly off, but she could see that teenage dignity wouldn't stand for probing. Perhaps there actually had been some sort of quarrel with her friend on the phone—or had the storm of tears come as a result of talking about Greville being so fat? It was difficult to tell. And maybe it was just teenage emotion, and an after-effect of running the high temperature which had brought her in here with her lungs congested and difficulty in breathing. Antibiotics and careful nursing had brought her out of that satisfactorily and she could, given the right circumstances, have been nursed back to health at home almost as easily.

Remembering how little Charly seemed to be visited, and remembering too with sudden vividness the concern of one Pensbury mother which had brought her in every afternoon to sit with *her* pneumonia child, Vicky knew that she had been wrong in her automatic criticism of private nursing. Children could be in desperate need of attention irrespective of the status of their parents. And then she had to remind herself quickly that it wasn't her job to get involved. It was one of the pitfalls of nursing children, and if she could remember how hard it had been to stay within the bounds of professional concern while nursing twenty children at once, it was obviously harder in the one-to-one situation operated by the clinic.

Simon would be perfectly entitled to give her a dressing-down if she started sounding over-possessive or over-critical about any patient. She had heard him being coldly caustic to one of the agency nurses for leaping to conclusions and had felt a startled quiver at the icy authority in his voice, which had made everyone within hearing almost jump to attention. It had shown Vicky yet another side of the man who was gentle and re-assuring with a sick child, humorous yet firm with a bouncy convalescent.

It was muddling to respect someone highly as a doctor while at the same time vowing not to take him seriously as a man, Vicky thought unwarily. She pushed the thought away with unusual haste. It was hard enough to feel that her life overlapped in too many directions, without confusing herself still further. She told herself very firmly, a little crossly, that it was just as she had thought at the beginning. There was too much to Simon Harraday altogether.

It was somehow even more annoying to go down for her coffee-break, with Charly settled back in bed, and be greeted by Clarice with, 'Hey, anyone know where the lovely Simon is today?'

'I expect Sister will know when he's coming in,' Vicky said coolly. 'Problems?'

'Only that I've just admitted one of his patients, and its glamorous mother was sulking a bit to find he wasn't here. Guess who it is, too? Jennifer Dane! Gave me quite a funny feeling to see her close up, because a bunch of us saw her on the stage only last night. And,' Clarice said, her eyes sparkling at the chance to impart a bit of gossip, 'guess who else was in the audience? And look-ing even dishier than usual? Our Simon, that's who!'

'Oh—really?'

'You might sound a bit more interested,' Clarice complained. 'I noticed him straight away—well, you can't miss him, can you?—even though he was down in the posh seats. *And* he was on his own.' She rolled her eyes, meaningfully. 'I bet he was there to take the leading lady out after the show, and you don't do that just because she's a patient's mum, do you? Besides, he wasn't looking that smooth for nothing! He had one of those really well-cut suede jackets on, and a silk shirt, and—'

'Were you examining him through a telescope?' someone asked with a chuckle. It was just as well, because Vicky had found herself with a sudden mad impulse to say that yes, she quite agreed, Simon did look nice last night because she'd noticed it when he went out. Or even to comment that he must have enjoyed the play because he was in a good temper at breakfast. She didn't know what had come over her, and covered her confusion by going over to fetch herself a cup of coffee from the percolator.

She knew who Jennifer Dane was, of course, because she was always turning up on television as well as on the West End stage, making her living, Vicky thought with unexpected sharpness, as much out of having a beautiful face as from her acting ability.

'I thought she was married to Marc Callender, isn't she? She must be married to someone if she's got a kid who's come in as a patient!' someone objected.

'They're probably divorced. Well, split, anyway. I read that somewhere. She was certainly making something out of Dr Harraday being such a great friend of hers and batting her eyelashes reproachfully because he wasn't around.'

'What's the child in for?' Vicky asked abruptly.

'Jimmy? Just an ordinary tonsillectomy. He's cute, a little dark-haired moppet—more like his dad than his mum. Some people have all the luck,' Clarice said with a sigh. 'Marc Callender, and then Simon—dunno which I'd rather have, really. What am I doing engaged to a redhead when I really fancy dark men?'

'What you really fancy is *men*,' two voices said in chorus, making Clarice give an unrepentant grin.

'Yeah, why not? An ordinary one for every day, and a bit of glamour on the side, to make a change. Hey, Jimmy won't be in for long, but I wonder if his dad will come and visit him as well as his mum—if he isn't away filming somewhere? That'd give us all something to swoon over, wouldn't it? Oh, by the way, Vicky, did you agree to go out with that lab technician who was trying to chat you up when we took those specimens down to the Path. Centre the other day?'

'*No*—he only looked about eighteen!'

'Might've had an older brother tucked away somewhere! You look a helluva lot prettier now you've got your hair done differently,' Clarice commented with her usual directness. 'Told you when I first saw it that you should've had it short at the front before! I s'pose you haven't remembered yet what the place was called where you had it done?'

The buzzer sounded abruptly, breaking up the group and giving Vicky the chance to do no more than shake her head. Somehow she had been unwilling to mention the famous name of Leon, which Clarice would be sure to know and remark on loudly. It would seem such an unexpected extravagance, almost a pretension, Vicky felt, to admit she'd had her hair done there, and she didn't want to go into it. Not into the whys and wherefores, certainly. It had been flattering to find that, even with her hair piled up under her cap, the new style had brought approving comments from the other nurses. It had been even more flattering, Vicky supposed, to find herself being chatted up immediately on sight by even a very young lab technician. And she had been aware of some interested male glances in the street too, let alone a wolf whistle from a building site. It was quite a revelation to find herself suddenly noticeable.

Not as noticeable as Jennifer Dane, of course. The actress had obviously stayed with her son for some little while to see him settled down, because she was coming down the stairs as Vicky started up them. It was odd, somehow, to see the real life version of someone so well-known, and to find her just the same—long honey-gold hair falling from a centre parting, huge limpid blue eyes, tip-tilted nose to give the face an enchanting cat-like delicacy.

Vicky stood aside politely, trying not to stare but noticing that Miss Dane's prettily-shaped mouth held a very discontented curve just at the moment. Then the curve changed abruptly to a wide, dazzling smile and the eyes which had looked past Vicky lit up. In a husky voice familiar from half a dozen television plays she said, 'Oh, there you are, at last!'

'Sorry, Jen, I meant to get here sooner but I was held up. Have you been here long?'

The deep voice with its velvety overtones was even more familiar, so it was no surprise to find Simon's tall figure appearing on the stairs as well. Since Jennifer Dane had stopped and Simon moved up to join her, Vicky found herself trapped in her polite stance against the wall as they greeted each other. The actress reached up to kiss the young doctor on the cheek. It was definitely more of a caress than a polite peck, Vicky found herself deciding crossly, feeling like a spare part who was invisible to the other two parties.

'Darling, I know you're busy, but I did say I'd come at ten,' Jennifer Dane was saying reproachfully, 'and I'm really supposed to be at a costume fitting. It's that stupid quick-change second act dress they still can't get right. Never mind, they'll just have to wait. Are you going to come up and see Jimmy now?'

'Yes, right now. Was he quite cheerful about coming in?' Simon asked, neatly turning the lovely young woman so that she went on up the stairs with him and

ignoring Vicky entirely. She obviously *was* invisible! She
was just acknowledging bitterly that anyone would be in
comparison with the lovely Jennifer, when Simon
proved her wrong by glancing back over his shoulder.

'Staff Nurse, don't go off duty before I've talked to
you about your patient, will you?'

'No, Dr Harraday.'

'Good. Sorry, Jen—you were saying?'

The two of them disappeared upwards. Vicky, follow-
ing more slowly, wondered why she should feel reduced
by his coolly impersonal tone. After all, he always did
treat her officially while they were at the clinic. On the
other hand, he often addressed the nurses by their
Christian names. She caught herself thinking acidly that
Simon obviously didn't want to be protected from the
interest of this particular lady, then shook herself, as if
by doing so she might shake herself into sense. Simon's
private life was absolutely nothing to do with her. She
was behaving just as if she was jealous!

The thought rocked her into stillness for a second
before she moved on quickly, her cheeks suddenly hot.
No, she wasn't! She wouldn't be so stupid—*hadn't* fallen
into the trap she was so carefully avoiding! She wouldn't
even think about it. If she did, she might have to
remember bitterly that there was no point in someone
like her being jealous of someone who looked like
Jennifer Dane.

Charly was wrapped in her own world behind the
headphones of a transistor she had brought in with her
and there was nothing that needed doing for her apart
from keeping an eye open until it was time for her lunch.
Vicky filled in the time by going on with the careful notes
she had started making on her patient since this morning
and then helping to sort the medicine cupboard. As in
any hospital, the supply of dangerous drugs kept in their
locked cupboards had to be checked from time to time.
Then, in an excess of busyness, she offered to relieve

someone who hadn't managed to grab a coffee-break. Suddenly she found herself missing the life of a large hospital ward where there were always jobs to be done or junior nurses to teach by example.

Sandra Smith, her relief, came on at one o'clock. Simon still hadn't reappeared. Vicky had been wondering whether she was supposed to go in search of him, but if he wanted to talk about Charly he knew where he'd find both patient and nurse—on the medical floor. She'd made a note that Charly had only pecked at her lunch, though Vicky had managed to get some of it down her by a good-humoured threat to remove the headphones if her patient couldn't eat *and* listen. Since then she had dealt with Charly's medicines and settled her down for a rest, but after she had handed over to Sandra she was stuck with being officially off-duty but still here. Sister Renfrew, Mary Cadogan's alternate sister-in-charge, tutted over it when the situation was put to her.

'He told you not to go off until he'd seen you? But he's not even in the building—he went out again after half an hour, with Jimmy Callender's mother! How trying the man is! And,' Sister said disapprovingly while Vicky was still digesting this information, 'how trying it also is that pretty women expect even doctors to act as a taxi service for them! Well, Nurse, I really don't know what to suggest, but since you're already half an hour late off duty I'm tempted to tell you simply to go!'

'I've made out some notes for him because he asked me to do some observation—but he did particularly say he wanted to speak to me.'

'When he does come back he's got a round to do. And I want to talk to him about tomorrow's operating list. He can't really have meant us to put in the Callender child after Mr di Angeli's skin-graft case, because that's going to tie up Theatre One for most of the morning—and he can't tell exactly how long he's going to be, with a facial birthmark like that. But we certainly don't want an ENT as well as an abdominal in Theatre Two, to give us *three* theatre teams tramping about!' Sister Renfrew wasn't nearly as placid as Sister Cadogan, in fact she often looked so sour that Vicky suspected her of being in danger of a peptic ulcer, though in spite of her temperament she was an efficient administrator. The theatre side was her particular pigeon and the difficult job of co-ordinating different visiting surgical teams usually ran like clockwork. She said sourly, now, 'I suppose it's going to be a case of special treatment to suit the parents rather than the patient or the nursing staff.'

'Ah, there you are, Sister. Staff Nurse.'

Simon's sudden appearance in the doorway was disconcerting enough to bring a swift flush running up under the skin of Sister Renfrew's thin face. His sudden appearance was, Vicky found herself thinking with resentment, a bit like the arrival of the demon king in a pantomime, though perhaps that was because he was frowning and not looking at all as if the company of his Jennifer had put him in a good mood this time.

'Do I gather you have a complaint, Sister?' he asked coldly.

'Staff Nurse Jardine should have been off half an hour ago, but you told her to wait until she'd seen you.' Sister was bridling a little, aware that he must have overheard her last remark and obviously wishing he hadn't. Vicky received a cool and unfriendly look from a pair of dark hazel eyes.

'You're in a hurry, Staff Nurse? You're off for the rest of the day, I suppose?'

'Actually I'm doing a split shift tonight, so I'm due back at five,' Vicky retorted, trying to sound meek, but not succeeding very well.

'Then you could have seen me later, couldn't you? I've been having some difficulty getting hold of Charlotte's GP, but he's coming in this afternoon. Hm, if you're off, you won't be present. Who's your relief?'

'Nurse Smith. I've made some notes.'

'You'd better give them to me then, and get off—since you're in such a rush.' He was still giving her an unfairly cold look as he held out his hand for the papers Vicky was holding, and it increased her feeling of resentment. He couldn't accuse her of being a clock-watcher! She'd been here all morning and quite available and it wasn't her fault if he'd chosen to go off and be a free taxi-service!

She looked at him with dislike, and opened her mouth to tell him sweetly that she didn't in the least mind being late off duty, thank you, but was interrupted by a bell ringing somewhere. Sister got up quickly to answer it, and as both the other two stood out of the way for her to pass, the moment was gone.

Simon came into the room and sat absently on the corner of Sister's desk, glancing down at the notes Vicky had handed him with a moody expression, then back up at her with the same coldness.

'You may not need to do your shift tonight—Dr Andrews wants me to discharge Charlotte today, that's why he's coming in to see me.'

'But she was only up properly for the first time today!'

'I'm aware of that,' he told her icily, as if her criticism had been for him. 'I may not have much choice if her own doctor wants her sent home with a nurse in attendance. No, not you. He has his own agency nurse in mind. Charly's parents are on the point of splitting up, apparently. Her mother's going off with someone else, and father's trying to cover the actual event by taking the children to Switzerland for a holiday. I can hardly object to that, on the pneumonia grounds. And no, Staff Nurse, I don't need you to tell me how relevant it all is! Let's avoid statements of the obvious, shall we?'

The caustic note in his voice was hardly fair, but Vicky's mind had fled to the frightened note in Charly's voice when she had said she wanted to go home.

'She *knows*,' she blurted out, but Simon cut her off scornfully.

'Yes, of course she knows, whether she's supposed to or not! Children aren't fools! And when you see most relationships nowadays,' he added savagely, 'it puts you off marriage. Now, you wanted to get off duty, didn't you? I apologise for keeping you.'

The expression on his face and the steely note in his voice didn't invite any answer. There wasn't, anyway, any answer Vicky could usefully make, or any protest, though several sprang to her lips about the trauma Charly must be going through and its possible results. If she made any of them she would be accused again of stating the obvious. It wasn't until she had got downstairs and was putting on her outdoor clothes that she felt a stirring of resentment again.

There was really no reason for Simon to take it out on her, or to give her that cold look of distaste as if she was responsible for all the ills of the world. True, she was the nearest person and he was obviously angry—but there had been an echo of other things in his remark about marriage. She wondered abruptly if he had been thinking about Marina. Or perhaps of Jennifer Dane, who was said to be in the middle of a divorce.

If Simon's private relationships held difficulties, that was still no reason for him to take his temper out on Vicky. She was nothing to do with any of it—just a substitute, a not-quite-sister, an occasional companion. And, while she didn't mind at all being the nearest person if he needed to take out frustrations and worries about a patient on someone, she was damned if she was going to be a sympathetic doormat to his moods about other women.

It was oddly like looking down the wrong end of a telescope to remember meeting Simon at Marina's wedding. How she'd disliked him, how she'd shed tears over Andrew. It was no comfort at all to realise that Andrew's image had faded so thoroughly from her mind.

It was even less of a comfort to realise whose image had replaced it. Vicky stood stock-still, shaken by the weakness which seemed to sweep through her. Now was not the moment to start remembering vividly how it felt to be kissed by Simon. She couldn't feel as if her whole life had been turned upside-down because of that, and his bossiness, and too much charm, and a fascination with his abilities as a doctor—and the simple, habitual pleasure of knowing she would see him across the breakfast table in the mornings! She made herself walk on, telling herself firmly and with as much humour as she could muster that it was ridiculous to imagine falling in love with a man just because you shared his breakfast toast.

It was only that he was different from anyone she had ever known before. It was only that she wasn't used to living at close quarters with someone so attractive. It was only that—she shut her mind hastily on any temptation to start listing the reasons why she might fall in love with Simon, and reminded herself very firmly that she'd decided only ten days ago never to take him seriously. She would do better to remember that, and why. She had had enough of comparing herself with Marina, and now there was Jennifer Dane . . .

In a sudden mood of defiance, Vicky decided that the only person she wanted to be was herself. And, since her off-duty time had been cut too short to make it worth going back to Belville Close, she would go shopping. Spending money seemed a satisfactory cure for being sore-hearted, and she toured the boutiques, splashing out on casual clothes which suited her new hairstyle and which certainly wouldn't stay hanging in the cupboard. By the time she went back to the clinic she was laden with parcels. She was also laden with good resolutions, most of which seemed to be about remaining cool, light-hearted, and totally uninvolved with any six-foot-three-inch, dark-haired, hazel-eyed, overbearing, changeable, and overwhelmingly attractive doctor she might happen to meet, even if she had to live with him.

She found that Charly had gone home and Vicky knew that she mustn't feel a stab of worry for the child. It was ironic to find which patient she'd been given instead, starting this evening—Jimmy Callender. Contrary to Sister Renfrew's fears, Jimmy wasn't for operation until the day after tomorrow, but it was to be Vicky who went up to theatre with him and specialled him afterwards. For tonight and tomorrow, she could get to know him as well as making sure that he wasn't brewing any infection to prevent the operation taking place as planned. She put away her parcels, checked the new shift timetable, and went to meet her new charge.

CHAPTER SIX

JIMMY was five and a half and since he greeted Vicky with the triumphant statement, 'I bin havin' *tests*', she could see that he wasn't at all daunted by being in hospital. He had very bright blue eyes under a pudding-basin fringe of dark hair, and an enchantingly cheerful personality which seemed quite unspoiled by having famous parents. If he was a little pale, and had a scratchy little voice which showed how often he had sore throats, he was otherwise bouncily healthy, and possessed of an outgoing friendliness which seemed to rest on the belief that everybody was going to like him, and he was going to like everybody. He had certainly inherited a lot of charm and Vicky couldn't help acknowledging that Jennifer Dane must be a good mother, however much her work must take her away from her child, to produce a little boy who felt secure enough to be so constantly friendly.

She was on until eleven and took a call from Jennifer Dane from her theatre to check that Jimmy had settled down all right. There had been another one from Jimmy's nanny, sounding both sad and apologetic about not being able to come and see him because she had symptoms of a cold—the reason why Jimmy had been brought in a day early.

Trundling back to Belville Close in a taxi at the end of her shift, Vicky took with her the picture of a small five-year-old sprawled in sleep next to his inseparable giant teddy bear and knew that, whatever mixed feelings she had had about being assigned to this particular patient, she was all the same looking forward to seeing Jimmy again for tomorrow afternoon's shift. Though to

judge by the number of nurses who had popped in to see
him out of curiosity and gone away again murmuring
that he was a love, he would probably be thoroughly
spoiled by the end of his few days at the clinic!

She was yawning a little as she paid off the taxi. It had
been a long day and what she needed was a cup of tea,
and then bed. As she carried her various parcels up the
stairs, she refused to remember that she hadn't seen
Simon since his icy bad temper in the middle of the
day—and with luck, she told herself with a sudden
return of moodiness, she needn't see him until quite late
tomorrow, and then only officially at the clinic, because
she needn't get up for breakfast if she wasn't on until the
afternoon shift.

It was disconcerting to follow that up by seeing him
immediately she walked into the sitting-room, where he
was lounging in a chair with one long leg hooked over the
arm, reading a book. It was even more annoying to find
that her thoughts seemed to have given her a peculiar
awareness of him, so that her heart gave a thump to see
him there looking absorbed and quite extraordinarily
handsome with one lock of dark hair falling untidily over
his forehead. Vicky dragged her eyes away from him
hastily and made for the kitchen, only to find herself
dropping her packages all around her. She heard Simon
move abruptly and say,

'Oh, hi. I didn't hear you come in. You're late, aren't
you?'

'I did the full shift instead of half a one.'

'Really? I thought you must have gone out somewhere.' He sounded quite casual about it, though he
could see, Vicky thought with irritation, that she hadn't
been out, since she was in uniform. He said something
else as she went into the kitchen, but she didn't hear
what it was because he had left a cupboard door open
and she bumped into it which made her swear crossly
under her breath. He'd also left the kettle sitting in the

middle of the table instead of putting it back in its usual place, and she muttered about that too. It might be his house, but he could at least be tidier! She filled up the kettle, found the flex which he had left in yet another unlikely place, and reached up to plug it in.

There was a loud bang, a sudden sting in her hand, and Simon's voice shouting, 'Vicky!' He was beside her before she had done more than blink in a dazed fashion, and she was aware of his hands jerking her bodily away from the plugs while she was still unthinkingly reaching out to the switch to turn it off again. 'Don't touch it, it might still be live!' he snapped, and then, 'Didn't you hear me say don't use the kettle? Are you all right?'

'Yes, I—think so.'

'Show me your hand.'

'It's all right.' It was still stinging a little, but as she turned it over, there wasn't even a mark. Vicky was suddenly aware that Simon was holding her quite unnecessarily tightly, and that she wasn't sure whether it was that or the mild electric shock which was making her feel peculiarly unsteady. 'I'm quite all right, and I'm sorry, I didn't hear you say anything about the kettle,' she said stiffly, trying to wriggle away from him. She didn't succeed because she was jammed up against the table. 'What's the—what's the matter with the thing, anyway?'

'I don't know, but if you weren't a complete *idiot* you'd have wondered why I'd spread it out all over the kitchen—just to stop anyone using it without thinking!'

'I just thought you were being untidy, as usual!'

'Being electrocuted doesn't seem to improve your temper, anyway!'

'Nearly electrocuting me doesn't seem to improve yours, either!' Vicky retorted furiously, knowing that it was unfair but suddenly wanting to take out an accumulation of anger on him. 'Would you mind letting me go? I really don't need artificial respiration!'

'More by luck than judgment! Why are women so stupid about electricity? You were just going to touch it again if I hadn't stopped you! And now I'm going to have to find the rubber gloves so as to take the whole thing apart again.'

'Oh, we're back with your male chauvinist attitudes, are we!' Vicky spat at him, somehow totally infuriated by the fact that his arms were still round her, and with such an extraordinarily protective feeling that it was making her feel weak at the knees. She felt a strange desire to burst into tears. Instead she glared up at Simon with complete ingratitude, and found herself saying waspishly, 'Maybe most of the women you know are stupid, but I happen to be a nurse, and practical, and apart from booby-trapped kitchens I'm perfectly capable of taking care of myself! So you can stop your Lord-High-Everything-Else attitudes and—and—'

'Cure you of hysteria?' Simon said, with his arms tightening round her, and a sudden gleam in his eye. Before she could do more than begin to guess at his intentions he had picked her up bodily, moved both of them out of the kitchen, put her down just long enough to change his grip on her—and then he was kissing her, soundly.

It was extraordinarily difficult to go on being angry with him. At least, it was until a moment later, when he lifted his head and said softly, caressingly, 'Better?' Vicky, who had been caught in a betraying, melting feeling that she wanted nothing more than for him to go on kissing her, sensed a mockery behind the single word which made her stiffen into defiance.

'Why on earth should that make me feel better?'

'Oh, I don't know, I thought it was going rather well. It's very difficult not to kiss you when you're spitting like an infuriated kitten. I'm only reacting normally,' Simon said reasonably, but with a maddening hint of laughter edging the soft velvet of his voice.

'Well go and react normally somewhere else, with someone else! Everyone else may swoon at your feet,' Vicky told him furiously, with exaggerated sarcasm, 'but I've told you before, *I don't!*'

'Sorry, I'm sure.' She saw the sudden anger in his eyes as he let her go and as he turned away she felt as if the temperature had suddenly dropped by several degrees. He said coolly over his shoulder, 'I'd forgotten how ardently you protect your virtue—or do I mean protect your neuroses? If you actually want a hot drink, boil some water in a saucepan.'

'No, I don't want anything after all, I'm tired, I'm going to bed!'

'Goodnight, then! Oh—are you going to leave these things all over the floor?'

Vicky walked past him wordlessly to collect up her forgotten parcels, and took herself away up to her bedroom in an equally cold silence. She was burning with resentment. It seemed better to fuel that than to let herself feel miserable. Why did he have to be so difficult to live with? Why couldn't she just take him lightly instead of letting him make her angry? She refused to let herself answer the questions and got into bed reminding herself that at least she wouldn't have to see him at breakfast.

Somehow, the next day, it seemed necessary to establish that she took Simon's behaviour as lightly as he did. After some thought she left a note propped on the kitchen table. It said, 'I apologise for screaming at you when you'd just saved my life—put it down to late shift work! P.S. Where have you taken the kettle, because I'll probably have more time to collect it than you will?' That seemed casual enough but semi-official too, and she decided rather abruptly that she'd go to a film after her shift this evening so as not to run into him as anything other than Dr Harraday at the clinic.

In fact she didn't see much of him there, although she

saw him in the distance talking to one of the visiting surgeons. It was noticeable that Jennifer Dane didn't see him either when she came in to visit Jimmy for an hour in the afternoon, because she asked Vicky rather petulantly where he was. The explanation that he was in conference over a patient who'd just been operated on was accepted with a wry shrug—at least Jennifer was knowledgeable enough to know that that was unanswerable, and she went back to playing snakes and ladders with Jimmy with a reasonably good grace.

Jimmy was a little moody after his mother had gone. He wanted Patricia, his nanny, and he wanted to go for a walk as he usually did—and he wanted to explore the whole clinic instead of staying in one part of it. Vicky kept him amused, knowing that it was hard for a child to accept being confined while he waited for an operation, and finding it touching that at five years old the little boy was prepared to accept the fact that grown-ups were 'busy at the moment' so he couldn't do all the things he wanted to do. Between them they bandaged his teddy bear for various illnesses, and decided to leave him with a smart throat-bandage to show that his tonsils were being treated as well as Jimmy's. It was more like being a nursery school teacher than a nurse, Vicky thought with amusement, even if in between treating the bear for appendicitis, infected ears, and a broken leg, she'd also managed to check on the arrangements for her patient's operation tomorrow and to note that the anaesthetist had been in to see him this morning.

Sandra Smith was acting as her relief again. Jimmy liked to know about everything, such as who was going to look after him, and when, and why, so Vicky explained that she was going to the cinema tonight and would see him again in the morning. She had in fact found another nurse to go with her, June Ellis, who had been commenting that *Easy Rider* had come back to the local Classic and asking if anyone else cared to come and watch it. Jimmy's reaction to the idea of a film was prompt.

·'Is it one with my daddy in?'

'No, love, he wouldn't be in this—it's a very old one. It was probably made when your daddy was about the same size as you are now!' Vicky was aware that the small boy was giving her a positively reproachful look and added hastily, 'I have seen films with your daddy, in, though. He makes a lot of them, doesn't he?'

'I'll probably be a sex symbol too, when I grow up,' Jimmy said with such careful solemnity that Vicky gave him a rapid hug to hide her laughter.

'I wouldn't be at all surprised. Now, shall we finish that story? Or are you going to read it to me, since you know it more or less by heart? We've just about got time before Nurse Sandra comes on, and then you're going to have your bath and go to sleep, aren't you?'

He liked live stories much better than television, Vicky had already discovered. They went through the story of an engine and an elephant together with Jimmy tucked companionably into the circle of her arm. He was busy telling her off for adding embellishments about what the people in the pictures might have said, so that neither of them heard the door open. It was Jimmy who looked up first, and it was only his sudden delighted bounce which told Vicky there was a third person in the room.

'Daddy!' he said in a scratchy squeak, and began to scramble out of her arms so rapidly that she had to catch him from falling. All at once, as the small boy launched himself across the room in a rush, she found herself meeting a pair of laughing blue eyes, as bright as Jimmy's, in a face which was familiar from the screen but subtly different. Then Marc Callender was bending down to swing his son up into the air and give him a warm hug.

'Daddy, Daddy, Daddy—you've come back, an' I'm having my tonsils, and this is my nurse that reads to me, and—'

'All right, Jims, don't strangle me!' Marc Callender kissed the little boy with obvious affection. The two faces close together had a remarkable likeness. 'Did you get my postcard with the camel on it? I've just got back, so I've come straight to see you.' He glanced across at Vicky, who was getting awkwardly to her feet. His warm, rueful smile showed exactly where Jimmy got all the charm from. 'Hallo, Nurse. I'm sorry if I'm interrupting something!'

'No, you're not—not at all.' It made Vicky a little shy to be meeting the 'sex symbol' face to face, just after hearing Jimmy call him that with youthful innocence. It was impossible not to respond to his friendly smile—though she noticed that he looked a little older off screen, and smaller too. He was a neat, compact man of no more than middle height, with the same dark hair as Jimmy's, the same blue eyes, but a face which was full of laughter lines.

Vicky wouldn't actually have classified him as a sex symbol for all his popularity because the parts he played were usually adventurous as much as romantic, and he wasn't classically handsome at all, though he made up for it by looking engagingly amiable and attentive. In fact he was looking so attentively at Vicky that she almost felt like blushing. 'I was just reading to Jimmy before it's time for his bath,' she said. 'He hasn't had his operation yet—it's tomorrow morning, but I expect you know that.'

'I do now. I didn't until I arrived.' There was a touch of grimness in his voice, though he covered it quickly as he turned his attention back to Jimmy. 'That's a nice important thing to be having, mate—your tonsils out! Just as well I got back, isn't it? I might have missed sharing your ice cream afterwards, otherwise! They *do* still give people ice cream after tonsils, don't they?' he appealed to Vicky hastily.

'Oh yes, always.'

'Just as well,' Marc Callender murmured, giving her a look of amused relief, 'or I might have said the wrong thing! Hey, Jims, what's your nurse called besides just "Nurse"?'

'This one's Nurse Vicky and she's nice. An' there's Nurse Sandra, and Sister, who isn't anyone's sister,' Jimmy informed him, wrinkling his brow at this puzzling circumstance, 'and Dr Harraday that Mummy calls Simon. And I had tests to see if my blood was red. And Mummy came this afternoon but she's busy now. But P'tisha can't come—'

'She sent you her love, though. She only can't come because she's got a cold. Anyway, *I'm* here now, so I can finish reading you that story instead of Vicky—if she doesn't mind!'

Receiving the full force of that exceptionally charming smile again, Vicky assured him that she didn't mind at all. Jimmy started chattering again, saying that he wanted to hear all about the 'filluming' instead of a story. But Marc Callender hushed him quietly with a gentle, 'In a minute, let me get a word in first,' which seemed to satisfy the child because he stopped at once, and leaned his head against his father's with such an open affection that anyone would have been touched by the picture they made.

'I've literally only just flown in,' Marc said, giving Vicky a rueful grin. 'We were filming in Tunisia and I didn't know anything about all this. Can I see this Dr Harraday a little later on? He's a new one on me. I'm sure everything's fine, but I'd just like to be put in the picture—I'm sure you can understand that!'

'Yes, of course. I'll make sure Dr Harraday knows you're here. I expect Sister's already told him,' Vicky assured him, and made her way to the door while father and son stood aside for her. If Marc Callender had been filming in Tunisia that explained why he was looking so brown, which suited him, though she found she couldn't look at him directly because it still made her shy to be at such close quarters with someone quite so famous. Just as she passed him he said appreciatively,

'*That's* a fine bandage your Teddy bear is wearing—did Vicky do that for him?'

The amusement in his voice made her feel faintly foolish to have been bandaging teddy bears. Jimmy said proudly, 'He's had broken arms and broken legs and broken *ears* today!'

'Goodness, he must have been falling down a lot,' Marc Callender said solemnly—and an unwary glance at him showed that his eyes were positively dancing with amusement. 'Come on, then, Jim—you get into bed, and I'll sit on the edge of it and tell you all about the camels! Let's give the prettiest nurse in London a moment's peace.'

Vicky, escaping, couldn't help an involuntary giggle. It was nice, she decided, even if totally untrue, to be referred to as the prettiest nurse in London. Marc Callender was quite unpretentious, and it was impossible not to like this one of Jimmy's parents better than the other, even if she had no valid criticism she could make of Jennifer Dane. As she walked towards Sister's office Vicky felt a sudden stab of fear that Jimmy, like Charly, would find himself between warring parents and suffer for it. But perhaps he wouldn't. He was very young, and so obviously well-loved. She tapped on Sister's door, which was closed for once, and it opened to reveal Simon as well as Sister.

They were finishing a discussion on the after-care for Mr di Angeli's skin-graft, which had apparently gone well, so Vicky stood waiting meekly until they had finished. Then she said, with cool efficiency, 'Jimmy Callender's father's here, Dr Harraday, and would like to see you, please?'

'Yes, I'd heard he'd arrived, that's good.' Simon gave
her an oddly sharp look, but all he added was, 'He's in
with Jimmy now, is he? I'll go in and see him in a
moment.'

'Is Jimmy's tonsillectomy still at ten o'clock
tomorrow, Sister?'

'Yes, Staff Nurse. Pre-med at nine. You'll be on right
through the day, so I'll give you a meal-relief.'

'Yes, Sister, thank you.'

'There shouldn't be any complications,' Simon said
absently, 'he's got a perfectly normal clotting time.
We've got the supply of Group A blood in case, haven't
we?' Sudden bleeding was the only real danger after a
tonsillectomy, as Vicky knew. Otherwise it was one of
the simplest operations. With proper theatre conditions,
and with no other children around him in a ward,
secondary infection would be extremely unlikely. She
had nursed enough post-operative tonsillectomies to
know what she had to look out for, but she waited to see
if Simon wanted to say anything else. He didn't, and she
could see Sandra Smith arriving at speed at the top of the
stairs, so she turned back to Sister Renfrew.

'I'm off now, Sister, unless you want me to do anything else? Nurse Smith's just arrived.'

'No, Staff Nurse, off you go.'

Sister Renfrew was always formal. It created quite a
different atmosphere in the clinic from the weekend
informality of Mary Cadogan who, being widowed,
didn't mind working through Saturdays and Sundays. If
Sister Cadogan had been on, Vicky thought, she might
have mentioned that she thought Mr Callender wasn't
best pleased to find his son about to be operated on
without his permission, but it wasn't altogether easy to
give personal opinions to Sister Renfrew with Simon
standing there. Jimmy's personal notes didn't actually
say that his parents were separated even though it had

been mentioned in the press. And Simon, she thought drily, was surely in a position to know what the family undercurrents were!

Vicky went off and changed into the clothes she had brought in with her and then went to the pictures with June Ellis, but even if the film was, according to June, one of the turning points in cinema history, she didn't find it interesting enough to stop her mind straying now and again towards the clinic. And Jimmy Callender, with his obvious affection for his father. And Simon. Surely Simon was putting himself in rather a difficult position by being involved with the mother of one of his patients? It didn't actually go against the Hippocratic oath because Jennifer wasn't his patient as well, but it could certainly make for an uncomfortable atmosphere now that Marc Callender was around too.

Vicky got back late, to a quiet house. She'd forgotten about her note and it wasn't until breakfast time, with Simon as usual ensconced behind a newspaper, that she discovered he'd written her an answer. Since his hand-writing was the habitual scrawl of most doctors he'd printed it in bold black capitals, and it was propped against the marmalade pot. It said, 'I forgive you. The kettle's at Harbottle's. P.S. Are we going to write to each other in future instead of talking? If so, remind me to take plenty of paper to the party!'

The vision of the two of them writing notes to each other at a party caught Vicky's sense of the ridiculous. Her chuckle made Simon lower the paper and give her a look of mock-caution. Her heart gave a sudden thump at the friendly, teasing gleam in his eyes and she paid rapt attention to the saucepan in which she was boiling water, saying calmly over her shoulder, 'Good morning. How long will the kettle be at Harbottle's, and do you want me to pick it up?'

'A week. Yes please,' he said meekly, and retired behind the paper again. From behind it he said, 'I'll get a bottle of wine for us to take to Chris and Terry's, by the way. Otherwise we'll find ourselves drinking Terry's home brew, and it's absolutely lethal!'

For a second, Vicky felt the impulse to tell him that she couldn't go to the party after all. Not with him. Surely there was some excuse she could give? Maddeningly, there wasn't. She could hardly claim that she had to work, when Simon would know as well as she did that, barring crises, her current patient would have gone home by then. She opened her mouth, then shut it again. Then, while she was still acknowledging bitterly that there was nothing she could say which might not make matters far too obvious, his voice came again from behind the newspaper.

'Incidentally . . . I don't have to warn you not to pay too much attention to Marc Callender, do I?'

'What?'

'He has quite a reputation,' Simon said coolly, invisibly. The paper rustled a little as he turned a page, but he still didn't reappear from behind it. 'And the mere sight of him seemed to set the night staff all a-flutter. I don't know what you thought of him, but—'

'I thought he seemed a nice man, and devoted to his son!'

'Then keep your thoughts on that level,' Simon advised. He seemed unconscious of the ice which had edged Vicky's voice, and of the flash of outraged anger in her green eyes too, as he folded the paper abruptly and stood up without looking at her. A moment later he had left the kitchen and she was alone, staring at the empty doorway in stunned disbelief.

How dare he warn her against Marc Callender, when he was so obviously friendly with the man's wife?

Vicky's mouth closed with a snap of anger. The warning was so ironic that she might have laughed if she hadn't been so furious. And what did he think she was, anyway—so silly and empty-headed that she'd fall in-

stantly in love with her patient's father just because he
was famous? And neglect her professional duty towards
Jimmy in the process?

Whatever else she thought of Simon, which was far
too much, she would have expected him to be fair.
Blackening Marc Callender, in the circumstances,
seemed a long way from fair.

There were a dozen things she might have said if
Simon had been there to hear them. It was just as well,
considering her status as his employee, that he wasn't.
When she left for the clinic half an hour later she hadn't
seen him again, and it ought to be have been a comfort to
feel that her opinion of him had plummeted. Instead,
she spent the short bus journey brooding.

She reached the clinic to find Jimmy being brave about
not being allowed any breakfast and Marc Callender
sitting with him again. It was unusual to allow a parent in
directly before operation unless there were special circumstances, but he had charmed Night Sister into letting
him come. It was impossible not to warm to a man who
understood how difficult it was for a five-year-old to see
why he couldn't have his usual cornflakes and milk, and
who was prepared to spend a lot of time and patience
distracting him. He left when he was told, too. He
paused for a word with Vicky outside his son's door as he
was going, showing an anxiety he had kept thoroughly
hidden from the child as he asked how long the operation would take.

She knew he had been told already by Simon but she
went through it again, giving him a reassuring smile as
she finished. 'It's only a very minor operation, you
know, under a light anaesthetic. He'll certainly be round
by lunch-time, though he'll be feeling a bit sore and
fretful, so it might be better if you waited a little while
before coming back again.'

'Jennifer wants to come this afternoon, so I'll come in
later.' He reached for a card, and scribbled some num-

bers on it. 'This is where I can be reached, just in case.'

The clinic already had the home number and this made it fairly obvious that the Callenders were living apart. Vicky hid a stab of sympathy for him, and smiled again as she accepted the card. 'There's really nothing to worry about,' she told him gently. 'And Mr Grantly's a very good surgeon—he does a lot of the ENT work here. I'll be going up to theatre with Jimmy and I'll be with him all the time afterwards, so he'll see a familiar face when he comes round.'

'He'll like that—Nurse Vicky who bandages his teddy bear for him.' Marc gave her his crinkly smile. 'Thanks for being so patient with me. I'll see you later, then.'

He gave her a rueful look as if to acknowledge that he knew he shouldn't worry, but would just the same, and touched her arm lightly before he walked away. He was a genuinely nice man, Vicky thought as she turned back to go into Jimmy's single ward, and she felt a curl of resentment again as she thought of Simon's comment. Then she put it out of her mind as she went to give Jimmy his pre-medication, and sit with him as he grew sleepy.

CHAPTER SEVEN

It was unnerving at first to walk into a crowded party wearing beautiful clothes and feeling that she'd arrived in a borrowed identity. Vicky was aware that there had been a flash of startled admiration in Simon's eyes when she came downstairs to join him for the party in the black satin trousers and top, with her hair floating in a cloud round her shoulders, and strappy black evening sandals giving her a few extra inches in height. He was looking extraordinarily handsome himself in an open-necked cream silk shirt and deep red corded velvet jeans which made him look quite unlike the formal Dr Harraday. Clarice, Vicky thought with an attempt at dry humour, would positively have passed out at the sight of him.

As they crossed the road to where music and laughter showed them the party was already in full swing, Vicky heard Simon say casually,

'We won't talk shop, by the way—okay?'

'I always try not to at parties—don't you?'

'Mm. It can be a temptation, though. Ah, they've left the door on the latch—looks as if we're supposed to walk straight in!'

It was a pity he had had to raise the subject of the clinic, because it took Vicky's mind instantly back to the week she'd just spent which was full of fragmentary impressions. Jimmy had gone home now, recovered even from the fretfulness of having a sore throat and back to a cheerful bounce, looking forward most of all to telling his nanny all about it because her cold hadn't, after all, developed to keep her away from him while he recuperated. Marc Callender and Jennifer Dane had gone on visiting him separately, Marc with a cheerful

patience and a habit of remembering all the nurses'
Christian names, Jennifer with an increasing nervousness. She saved all her charm for Simon. On one occa-
sion her agitation rubbed off on Jimmy and made him
start to cry and hold out his arms for Vicky rather than
his mother. Vicky wondered if she'd complained about
it. She'd be bound to leave out the fact that she'd just
snapped at the little boy that no, his nurses couldn't
come and visit him when he went home. Certainly Simon
had given Vicky a sharp glance when he looked in
unexpectedly some time later. Marc Callender had been
there by then, behaving with his usual niceness. Behind
the cool formality with which Simon treated his young
patient's father, Vicky could sense a wariness between
the two men. It gave her an instant feeling of depression,
though she hid it carefully. She told herself, too, that the
depression was for Jimmy, and for Marc. If ever a man
deserved an uncomplicated relationship with his own
child, he did.

She had seen little of Simon at home over the last few
days. They had both been busy, and it was surprisingly
easy to avoid someone, even in a small house, if you
were determined to do so. When they had met, they had
in fact talked shop, because Simon had caught her with
the joyful news that a kidney had come up for Sebastian.
In fact the young boy was in Hammersmith Hospital
right now, and the entire clinic staff were keeping their
fingers crossed for him after an apparently successful
operation.

Vicky tore her mind away from memories of work.
Cinderella had come to this party, and Cinderella was
going to enjoy it. And not necessarily with Simon—
there must be other people to talk to. She gave Chris a
deliberately wide smile when the other girl appeared out
of the crowd saying, 'Hi, both—hey, I like the outfit!
Come and meet some people!' Then she had to try not to
wince when Chris drew them into the nearest group and

announced them with, 'This is Simon and Vicky who live opposite.' Simon-and-Vicky—that was some fantasy.

The house was built on the same pattern as number ten, but decorated so differently that it felt quite strange. Chris and Terry seemed to go for bright colours, the minimum of low modern furniture and hanging plants all over the place. The party was taking over almost every part of it including the garden where Terry was operating a barbecue. It wasn't difficult, Vicky found after a while, to drift away from Simon, because a surprisingly large number of the male guests seemed keen to meet her.

Nor was it difficult to get into conversation because she only had to ask people what they did. Half of them were in television like Chris, and most of the others worked with computers—Terry, she gathered, was in computers. Her pleasant, bearded host told her so himself while offering her a charred sausage and giving her a friendly grin while he said it was nice to meet her properly at last. Then he spoiled things by telling her cheerfully that if she'd lost Simon, he was last seen in the kitchen trying to teach the mynah bird to say something evil. That made the fair young man who had brought her out into the garden after an animated discussion about home video look noticeably disappointed. It was flattering, but it was annoying too, particularly when she was aware that she lost him a little later because he went in search of someone unattached.

The Simon-and-Vicky illusion seemed determined to follow her around the party, she decided some time later with a spark of resentment. No matter how much care she took to be raptly attentive to someone else whenever he hove into view, no matter how often she manoeuvred herself out of a room if she saw he was in it, it seemed to be generally known that she was 'with' Simon. There was even one direct comment about it which both startled her and made her grimly thoughtful. She hid it behind a light amused shrug, and went on trying to look as if she was enjoying herself.

She ought to have been enjoying herself. She talked, laughed, danced, and was aware of receiving both interest and admiration. An increasing number of people crammed into the small house. Vicky chatted to girls who asked her enviously if she ever had to diet, men who wanted to know if she'd ever done any photographic modelling and various people who seemed surprised to hear she was a nurse rather than in some branch of the performing arts. There wasn't anywhere to sit down, so people circulated or danced or sat on the stairs. Terry's home brew, which Vicky deliberately sampled, didn't taste lethal at all but light and fruity. The music got louder and the barbecue was abandoned when the sausages and hamburgers ran out.

At some point, a ginger-headed young man who was dancing with her asked her wistfully if she had a sister, the look in his eyes making it plain that he intended it as a compliment. Vicky's heart gave a sudden unwary stab, and she felt an abrupt impulse to tell him that actually she was the spare sister. She didn't though, because it was obvious he would have taken it as immediate encouragement, and he wasn't really her type!

She glanced involuntarily across the noisy, crowded, smoky room to where she had last seen a certain very tall red-trousered figure, feeling suddenly and defiantly that if everyone believed she was Simon's property she might just as well have spent the party with him, instead of tiring herself out avoiding him. It seemed silly to waste the chance. She felt an ache of emptiness to discover that he wasn't where she'd last seen him, dancing amicably with the beautiful Chris. All at once she wanted him with such unnerving force that it was like being shaken to pieces. She was abruptly sick of the whole evening, even of the discovery that she had her share of the family beauty after all. At least half a dozen men had made it plain they thought so, but she didn't want any of them. She wanted Simon.

She tried to wriggle further away from the ginger-headed Roger, who seemed to be taking her silence for consent to close in on her as the music took on a slow, sensuous beat. He was more than a little drunk, she thought irritably, as her movement made both of them stumble over a low table sticking out from the side of the room.

A pair of strong arms fielded her neatly from behind, and she was detached from Roger's grasp and turned round to land with a thump against a broad chest. A deep familiar voice said above her head, smoothly, 'I think it's time I reclaimed you. Sorry, mate, but I don't seem to have seen her all evening, so I reckon it's my turn!'

The tone, Vicky thought dazedly, was friendly enough, but had distinct overtones of telling somebody to back off. It was enough to take her breath away to wish for something and then have it granted immediately, but with instant contrariness she felt a flash of resentment. She looked up swiftly, green eyes meeting hazel ones, and found enough breath to say,

'Did you think I needed rescuing, or something?'

'No, did you? I just thought it was time you danced with me for a change. You seem,' he said lightly, but looking down at her with an odd intentness, 'to have been enjoying yourself.'

'Yes thanks, I've been having a lovely time. Have you?'

'Not much, but then I'm not very party minded. I thought we might go home soon, what do you think?'

Vicky felt inclined to suggest that *he* went home and she stayed, because that would make the true position between them clear. Alternatively, since his arms were wrapped round her and she was weakly, meltingly aware of his body moving gently against hers to the slow beat of the music, she wanted nothing more than to rest her head against his shoulder and enjoy dancing with him. After all it was only what everyone would expect. She found herself doing it, her cheek nestling into the curve of his shoulder as if it belonged there. Simon turned his head to rest against her hair and a shiver of pleasure went through her as his arms tightened round her, one hand moving, as if absently, in a stroking curve down her back. She felt his lips brush against her temple, and the deep voice said softly,

'That's better. I don't seem to have seen you for far too long, or only in the distance. You're looking very fanciable tonight. Very beautiful, too. Did I remember to tell you so?'

'Plenty of other people did.' The words came out involuntarily, though she didn't want to quarrel with him. She wanted, she realised suddenly, to make him jealous. The Simon-and-Vicky fantasy seemed to have taken her over. She stirred uncomfortably, not wanting to remember how untrue it was. All the same she heard herself going on, in a voice which seemed half-drugged by the sensuality of the music, or perhaps by the amount she had drunk. 'Lots of people fancied me, why not? Lots of people who'd never seen me as Marina's little sister, but as *me*!'

'You're not still competing, are you?'

'No, that was just the point I was trying to make!' It was a pity, but she was waking up. The shivery feeling which came from the magnetism of being held close against him was turning into a glow of anger. 'It's you that turned it into a competition, isn't it? You that—that remodelled me? You shouldn't sound so surprised that you suddenly find me fanciable—you took enough trouble over it!'

His chest rose sharply against her on an indrawn breath. 'So you *have* been avoiding me all evening! I wondered why—or if I was imagining it. It seemed a bit too pointed for imagination, though, particularly after Chris asked me politely if we'd quarrelled! It's about time we sorted out—'

'Such a pity Jennifer couldn't come,' Vicky said abruptly. She was miserably aware that she *was* quarrelling with him, low-voiced and wrapped up together in such intimacy amongst the crowd that she could feel his heartbeat mingling with hers. If anyone noticed, she thought angrily, they could take it as a lover's tiff. 'Surely she could have come along after the theatre? It must be pretty late by now—'

'What do you mean by that?'

'Jennifer. You know, *Jennifer* . . . the lady you're currently interested in!'

'I don't know what you've been drinking,' Simon said coldly against her ear, making sure she didn't move away from him by increasing his apparently affectionate hold on her, 'but it seems to have given you some very funny ideas. And when we get home you can explain them. You—'

'I just thought it was a pity that you had to be here with the wrong partner. And I'm not sure that I like being a stand-in,' Vicky threw at him recklessly. She lifted her head from his shoulder to glare up at him, which was difficult from such close quarters. 'I'm not sure that I like being a stand-in for *anyone*, for that matter! I suppose it doesn't occur to you how much you've been cutting the ground from under my feet?' She saw the startled look in the dark eyes slanting down at her, but she rushed headlong on. 'Oh, and by the way, I did discover why you felt I'd be such a useful protection while you were between attachments. Someone actually told me, and it made your position quite clear!'

'*What* did someone say to you?'

'It was that young man with a chip on his shoulder— the scruffy one. He said if I was shacked up with Harraday Electronics I wouldn't be interested in him, because he was merely a humble computer programmer. And I can quite see,' Vicky said with heavy sarcasm, 'that if you're one of *those* Harradays you might easily get chased. All that money as well as being handsome and successful!'

'If you're determined to pick a fight with me about absolutely everything we won't do it here,' Simon said between his teeth. To Vicky's chagrin, he shut her up in the most effective way possible. His mouth, from only a few inches away, came down hard on hers. She wanted to twist away but it was impossible when he was so much the stronger, and she could feel the hard male anger in him, the bruising tension of his muscles as he crushed her against him, the tumultuous race of both their hearts. And, as her knees seemed to buckle and she was filled with a yearning longing, she knew unwarily that she had wanted him to do exactly this . . .

She was aware of the anger in Simon melting, of his muscles relaxing a fraction so that his strong hold became more of a caress than an imprisonment. His lips moved against hers more gently, catching her in a sweet magic. She wasn't aware that the music had stopped, to be replaced with a light buzz of conversation while somebody found another tape, until he removed his mouth from hers and murmured softly against her ear,

'That's a much better way to pass the time—isn't it?' He went on, in the same velvet caressing tone, 'And I'm not sure I mind at all if I've been cutting the ground from under your feet.'

It was a pity he had to remind her—the magic suddenly died. Vicky found that she had pushed herself away from him in a movement sharp enough to catch him off guard, and that a combination of frustration, rage and misery were boiling up in her as she glared up at him. 'I've had enough,' she said frostily, 'I'm going home. You can stay!'

She was aware of one or two heads turning towards

them. She didn't care, and it only made her angrier when Simon caught her wrist in a hard grip to keep her beside him. 'I said I'm going,' she told him pointedly, not bothering to lower her voice, 'so will you please let go of me?'

The music started again with a sudden loudness which somehow made it easier to twist her arm away from him, turn, and make for the door. The people around seemed no more than a blur. Vicky found herself down the stairs and opening the street door before she was aware of her own rapid flight, or of the fact that she had almost tripped over several couples sitting on the stairs and at least two people had called out goodnight after her. The cool night air stung her burning cheeks. Party noises and the muffled beat of music seemed to fill the entire street as she picked her way across the road on legs which seemed suddenly unsteady, and her hands didn't seem to belong to her as she fumbled in her tiny evening bag for her key. The long cream ruffle at her wrist seemed to keep getting in the way. She didn't want to acknowledge that she was shaking as much from misery as from anger—nor to remember that she had just picked a public quarrel with Simon, in front of his friends, when all she really wanted to do was . . .

A tall form loomed suddenly on the doorstep behind her and a hand came over her shoulder to insert a key, turn it, and push the door open. Simon's voice said, in a quite murderously icy tone,

'There you are. Now let's go in!'

'You don't have to leave the party—'

'I stayed long enough to thank Chris and Terry for having us,' he said pointedly. Then, as if he was tired of having his way blocked across his own doorstep, he pushed Vicky inside and slammed the door behind both of them.

She fled instinctively upwards. In fact he more or less bundled her up the stairs, coming so close behind her that she nearly tripped and heard him mutter an angry exclamation as he steadied her. He was still holding on to her when they reached the sitting-room, and before she knew what was happening she found herself pushed hard, so that she came up against an armchair and sat down in it with a thump. She blinked breathlessly, and gazed up at him with a conflict of emotions, of which resentment was uppermost.

'Now we'll talk. Privately, here—if you're sober enough!' He was standing over her like an angry inquisitor, his eyes darkened with scorn. Six foot three of muscular rage, as handsome as the devil with his winged eyebrows and that curling, sardonic mouth. She tore her eyes away from him hastily and shook her head to try to clear it. 'If that means no,' he said icily, 'you can think again. Or if it means no, you're not sober enough, I'll dunk you under the kitchen tap.'

'Who the hell do you think you are?' Vicky sparked at him, her eyes flying up to his face in outrage.

'A man way out of patience. And I'm not used to being publicly put down, either. I like my fights private—'

'And your women willing. Yes, I remember!'

'Shut up, or I might change my views on that. You're enough to—but we'll leave that for the moment. Now. First. What was all that about Jennifer?'

'Isn't she your—?'

'She isn't my anything. No, I'll correct that. She's a friend. A friend,' Simon repeated coldly as Vicky opened her mouth, 'who happens to be having matrimonial problems. Of which I am *not* part. And you should know better than to invent damaging gossip!'

'I didn't invent it! Someone said—and you obviously know her very well!'

'I'm her child's doctor. I'm also an old friend, an acquaintance, until recently. People confide in doctors, it goes with the territory. Jennifer happens to be going through a bad time. I was there, so she talked to me about it. I don't propose,' Simon said coldly, 'to discuss her problems because they were told to me in confidence. But I don't like gossip, and if you didn't invent it you should at least have the sense not to repeat it! And considering some of the things you've heard me say, I should have thought that you'd know I don't believe in *anyone* getting mixed up in other people's marriages!'

'Sh—should I?' Vicky was gazing at him wide-eyed, mesmerized by the angry face so far above her. He wasn't in love with Jennifer—the knowledge seemed to sing in her blood. She wanted to blurt out that she wasn't in love with Andrew any more either; that she had grown out of imagining she was; that his last, sardonic, remark hadn't been necessary. Then she remembered the rest of it, and her heart seemed to sink down through her stomach with a miserable thud. She was still a stand-in. Marina's stand-in. She gave Simon an abruptly hostile look, and swallowed the apology she'd been about to make. 'Well?' she said sharply.

'Well what?'

'Have you finished lecturing me? Because if you have, I'd like to go to bed!'

'No, I'm not through with you yet! There's still that other accusation you levelled at me. I can't help what family I was born into, any more than anyone else can—and it's my uncle who's Harraday Electronics, not me! Just to make matters thoroughly clear,' Simon said on an angry breath, 'I may be part of the same family, but I had to beg the money to open the clinic. Why else do you think I had to put the Harraday name on it? Self-advertisement? And while you're in the line of making snide remarks about my being rich as well as successful, I work pretty hard for what I get, or hadn't you noticed? And what would you suggest I should have done with the advantage of starting out with money behind me? Sat on a beach somewhere twiddling my toes, instead of trying to do something useful?'

'No, you'd have got bored to death. And besides you're a good doctor.' Vicky caught herself up on the involuntary honesty of her answer and remembered she was angry with him. 'But maybe I don't like being told I'm "shacked up" with you,' she told him with hostile dignity, 'and you might have told me, because if I'm going to be accused of being a gold-digger, I might at least know what I'm supposed to be digging! Added to that, I'm *not*, and I got very tired of people telling me all evening where to find you, as if I was a—a piece of lost property!'

'Ah yes. This is where I'm supposed to say I'm sorry I spoiled your evening.' Simon's face was a sardonic mask. If Vicky hadn't been miserably aware that it wasn't true, she might almost have thought he minded her rejection of him. With a sudden flash of longing she hoped it might be true, but he was going on. 'I stopped you having a good time and you don't like being remodelled—and I'm sure you can think of half a dozen other things to throw at me, given time! I'll tell you what! Go back to the party. Pin a notice on you saying "I don't belong to Simon Harraday". Or shall I give Chris a ring, and ask her to pass the word round? Or if you can tell me who it was you particularly fancied, I can ask her to put the word in that direction! Go on—what are you waiting for?'

It was almost as if he really was jealous. Vicky gazed at him wide-eyed. Suddenly she wanted to burst into tears. She wanted him to pick her up and comfort her, to kiss her as if he really meant it, to hold her as he had held her at the party during that one short dance which was all she wanted to remember. Her lip trembled dangerously, and she burst out,

'Oh go away and leave me alone!'

'With pleasure,' he bit out furiously and turned on his heel, making for his bedroom door. Over his shoulder he said, sounding singularly short of breath, 'But I'll tell you one thing—I thought Marina was the most temperamental girl I'd ever met, but you're worse! You should carry a public warning about with you! Both of you!'

His door crashed shut behind him with enough force to rattle the furniture. Vicky stared after him for a shaken moment and then she was out of the chair and scuttling up the stairs for the haven of her bedroom. Marina again—*always* Marina. She slammed her own door, stood stock-still, then flung herself in the direction of the bed. And then she did burst into tears, burying her face in the pillow to stifle her sobs. It didn't matter at all that she'd been wrong about Simon and Jennifer Dane. And it didn't make any difference that she, Vicky Jardine, had seen herself reflected in a lot of people's eyes tonight as someone who could be attractive in her own right. She was desperately, despairingly in love with the one man who would always compare her with Marina.

Morning brought calm and a headache which she told herself was a hangover. And a long, free day.

She heard Simon in the shower. Some time later, to give him time to have gone out, she got up herself. She pulled some clothes dispiritedly out of her wardrobe, some of the new ones. She might as well stick to the new Vicky personality. Inspecting herself in striped dungarees, a T-shirt, and with a ribbon tied at random in her hair, she decided that she looked like Noddy; but who cared? At least Simon hadn't bought them; they were her own choice. She was only going to do the housework anyway. And maybe go for a wander on Hampstead Heath later with nothing but her own thoughts for company. She pulled a face to try and cheer herself up and drifted downstairs. Simon would probably have taken the Sunday paper out with him, so she'd have to go out and buy one—if she could be bothered.

It was a shock to see him sitting in the sunlit kitchen in his usual place, with the debris of a late breakfast spread out in front of him. Vicky stiffened. He hadn't heard her soft-footed approach, and she felt inclined to flee. She had spent most of the night telling herself to be sensible, but the sight of that familiar dark head, just visible as usual above a newspaper, did disastrous things to her resolutions. Oh, why did she have to love him so much?

She didn't want to hear the cold greeting he would give her, if he gave her any at all. Most particularly, she didn't want him to see her standing here with her heart in her eyes. She turned away sharply. As she did so, she heard his chair shift, and before she could take another step she heard the deep voice say, on a calm, almost cheerful note,

'Hi. I wondered how long you were going to sleep. Am I in your way?'

'No . . . no, of course not.'

She had to go into the kitchen then. His eyes had gone back to the paper but he had folded it now, so she couldn't even hide by staying the other side of it. She satisfied herself by not looking at him, as she fiddled about boiling water for coffee and deciding with revulsion that she didn't want anything to eat. She thought he was intent on what he was reading, but a moment later that was denied as he said pleasantly,

'Am I allowed to say you look nice?'

'Do I? Thanks.'

He was sounding as normal as if last night's quarrel had never happened. Perhaps it just didn't mean anything, to him. Vicky drank her coffee standing up because that was a good way to keep her back to him without looking as if she was deliberately doing it. She stared out of the window as if totally absorbed by the view, although it looked much the same as usual, and tried to keep her mind fixed on nothing but the thought that summer would soon be over. She heard Simon stir, and then he said, quite casually,

'We're both free today, aren't we? Would you like to drive somewhere?'

'I'm afraid I'm going out all day. Pre-arranged date,' Vicky said hastily, apologetically. Surprise had made her turn round to look at him, and she thought his mouth tightened a little. Somehow that made it necessary to elaborate the lie and to sound as politely friendly as possible. She seized on the first place which came into her head. 'I'm going to Kew Gardens—'

'You're not obliged to give me chapter and verse. Have a nice day, then.' Simon stretched, taking his eyes away from the newsprint at last to give her a brief glance. 'I think I'll spend the day working on that paper I'm supposed to be writing on the correlation of infant jaundice with later medical conditions. It's time I got down to it, really.'

He stood up, gave her a cool, impersonal glance, and wandered out of the kitchen. His voice had been perfectly amiable. Vicky was left with a sudden, passionate longing to have accepted the invitation. Why, oh why had she rushed into invention?

CHAPTER EIGHT

WORK caught her in its comforting arms and kept her busy enough to leave no time for reflection, for she was allocated to another of Mr Grantly's cases. The child, whose adenoids were removed at the same time as his tonsils, wasn't one of her most pleasant cases. He was spoiled and whiny and generally unco-operative, with parents who, like their eleven-year-old son, looked for things to complain about. It was a relief when he went home, though less of a relief when her next patient turned out to be a bouncing hyperactive in for a complicated operation on the hyper-thalmus.

It seemed that Mr Grantly had asked for her to be given his cases, which was flattering but a little disconcerting when Vicky preferred, if she'd been given the choice, to do less of the surgical side. It was clinic practice for the Nurse to go right into theatre for the operation so as to be thoroughly knowledgeable about everything that had been done. Vicky had done her share of theatre-work in training, and found it interesting, but had known it wasn't going to be her choice. Not just because of the long hours spent bundled up in boots, gown and mask, or because of the endless counting and sterilising of instruments, but because she preferred her patients conscious and as interesting individual personalities. Specialling was post-operative too, of course, and gave her both sides, but she would still rather have been watching over a medically ill child than standing in theatre waiting to retrieve one who'd had surgery.

Simon, on the other hand, didn't seem to be busy. At least, he was as far as work was concerned, but he seemed to be around the house a lot when Vicky was in it. He was still treating her as pleasantly as if they'd never hurled fury at each other. In fact he was being unusually calm and amiable. They even had some interesting medical discussions across the kitchen table, talking shop because they found the subject absorbing.

It was almost as if they were starting all over again from scratch, Vicky thought moodily. She ought to have been able to congratulate herself on the way she was able to respond to him without showing her feelings, just as if he was an ordinary acquaintance instead of the man she lay awake over at nights with a confused, aching longing.

She found herself with an odd restless discomfort whenever they shared breakfast or spent a quiet evening in the same room in front of the television. It was a wry thought to realise that she missed Simon's teasing which had annoyed her so much, the gleam of challenge in his eyes when he said something outrageous. Nowadays he was pleasantly civil. If he occasionally told her she looked good in something she was wearing, it was casually said and didn't provoke her to disagree with him. He was just as likely to break the silence to tell her something about one of their cases—such as the fact that Sebastian was still doing well after his kidney transplant.

It was idiotic to feel the urge to pick a fight with him—just to see what would happen.

Her nursing duties temporarily slackened off when she was given a quiet diabetic child to nurse, and Vicky suddenly found herself with a lot of free evenings. It seemed necessary to be sociable instead of staying at home, so Vicky went out with June Ellis again, on a foursome date which included the other girl's brother and tried not to feel that it was an exceptionally dull evening. Then she went to a film with Lannie, the Filipino nurse, who was small, sweet and practical. Clarice flung her a cheerful invitation to come down to Earls Court for a fish-and-chip party with 'the gang' in a couple of days' time, and she accepted that too. Since

Clarice had prefaced the invitation by telling Vicky that she intended introducing her to some really wow Australians, the evening ought to have been promising. It might even cure her, Vicky thought drily. She went, and came back wondering why it hadn't been any cure at all to be hugged by someone just as large as Simon if twice as noisy. She'd been greeted with open arms, anyway, and it was comforting to be told enthusiastically that she was a 'really beaut little Sheila', by a blonde, rugger-playing giant who was really quite handsome in his way.

It was just that he wasn't Simon. And Simon had had to choose that same night to offer to take her to the theatre. He'd suggested it casually, saying he'd got tickets for the Barbican and would she like to come? Vicky had found herself stammering,

'I would have loved to, but I promised to go out—'

'Okay. Don't worry about it. I just remembered that you'd never been—but perhaps you have by now. Someone gave them to me,' he said lightly over his shoulder as he went back into his bedroom, from which he had emerged to catch her as she was leaving to go on duty.

He wouldn't ask her again, she thought with a frustrated surge of longing. She tried to crush it down as she went out to catch the bus. Why did it have to be the same night as Clarice's party? And why hadn't she just abandoned Clarice's party—as the other girl would certainly have expected her to do, if she'd known about the alternative!

The gloomy thought went on duty with her and was still there next day, too, when she woke up with a buzzing head and a resolution not to drink Australian beer in future. Life, she thought sourly, was not only unfair, it would also turn her into an alcoholic if she wasn't careful. She put on her uniform for the afternoon shift and went to make herself several cups of strong coffee.

Simon had left a gossipy tabloid newspaper lying

about the kitchen—unusually, considering he read *The Times*—and she picked it up idly. A paragraph caught her eye, making her look more closely. It announced that Jennifer Dane, the well-known actress, was planning to marry the leading man in her current West End comedy. There was a blurb about Jennifer's television career, a mention of her six-year marriage to Marc Callender and a brief reference to Jimmy. Vicky tried not to feel an undue concern for Jimmy, who would probably settle down to having a visiting father with the same cheerfulness that he accepted having a father who was often away working. She tried not to feel sad for Marc, too, because theatrical divorces were commonplace and none of it was her business. All the same, she wondered if Simon had left the paper for her on purpose as a pointed proof.

She had believed him anyway, and it was a pity if he'd left the paper there because he thought she hadn't. Things were muddled enough between them without that.

She felt a sudden, unexpectedly defiant wish to fight for what she wanted instead of sitting around brooding about it. Marina was *married* and well out of reach, she told herself. It was ironic as well as surprising to find herself thinking that if she could just give up so easily she must be as spineless as Simon had once accused her of being! She was perfectly well aware that, having taken the trouble to turn her from a moth into a butterfly, even he found her attractive. And here she was under his feet yet scarcely saying a word to him.

She felt a confused knowledge that the moth hadn't quite learned how to lure someone's full attention. And that it was better not to start wondering how to try when she was just going on duty and would have to face him in her nurse's identity some time during this afternoon.

Her diabetes child had gone home now, and she was down to act as relief for the nurse specialling a three-

year-old Cypriot girl with the mouth-tangling name of
Elena-Maria Papasstheniou, who had been operated on
two days before to correct a congenital foot malforma-
tion. Vicky kept her mind firmly on remembering what
she knew about talipes equinus, or old-fashioned club
foot, and on trying to bring a smile into the solemn dark
eyes of little Elena. All the same she couldn't help
watching Simon with an oddly unsteady feeling in her
stomach as he came in to sit on the edge of Elena's bed
and broke the little girl's gravity by teasing her gently in
apparently fluent Greek. At least it sounded fluent to
Vicky, though the bilingual Elena told him with delight
that he was saying everything wrong.

Simon wasn't at the house when she got back for the
evening. His answering service rang for him, but when
Vicky couldn't give them any help, said not to worry,
they had several other numbers to try for him. Vicky
went back to wondering, with a confused uncertainty
which seemed remarkably mixed up with determination,
how she could set about making a change in her relationship with Simon.

When he wasn't there in the morning it gave her a
suddenly sick feeling. She went in to the clinic telling
herself that doctors—even private doctors—could get
called out all night. She found herself walking into the
clinic with June, who immediately started telling her that
her brother had suggested another foursome date. June
was still going on about it with a cheerful ignorance of
the impatience Vicky was concealing, as they went
towards the rest-room to hang up their coats. But
although she jumped, she wasn't nearly as disconcerted
as Vicky by the sudden interruption which cut across her
speech.

'Staff Nurse Jardine, you'll have to leave your private
life for the moment,' Simon's voice said from the stairs,
sounding coldly angry. 'I want to talk to you. Be in
Sister's Office on the first floor in five minutes.'

'Goodness, I wonder what you've done?' June's whisper turned to a squeak as he vanished. Vicky, feeling suddenly very shaken, was wondering the same thing. Had she made some terrible mistake, or what . . . ?

She found out what when she she was making for Sister's Office, in well under the required five minutes. She ran into Clarice, flashing upstairs with an armful of linen. The other girl paused to impart some breathless information, keeping her voice for once low and with her usual bounce diminished into an uncharacteristic seriousness.

'Hey—don't take on if our Simon seems in a vile mood. I've seen him like this before, and it isn't personal. It's because of Twin—'

'Sebastian? Oh, don't say it's all broken down!'

'No, Sebastian's fine. It's Ben—the other one. Admitted late last night. Poorly,' Clarice said, using the hospital understatement which sent Vicky's heart cold. 'Think I'm probably going to be nursing him, 'cos I've been sent for.'

'Me too.'

'Yeah? *And* Deb Adam. Looks like it might be the three of us round the clock, then.'

'What is it?' Vicky asked quickly, her mind flying to accidents of different kinds.

'Viral meningitis,' Clarice said quietly. 'Spinal lumbar puncture last night, diagnosis confirmed this morning. Yeah, I know. Look, I'll see you up there in a moment, when I've dumped this stuff.'

She shot away. Vicky, with all her personal concerns forgotten, hurried on up the stairs. Viral meningitis—Ben? He might die, or end up brain-damaged . . . How had he managed to catch it? And, oh God, what must the twins' parents be feeling, just when they'd been given the hope of two healthy, normal sons?

The conference in Sister's Office was detailed, terse, and carefully undramatic. Simon might be speaking in his coldest voice, with an expression on his face which made Vicky's heart give one flip of sympathy in the middle of her concentration, but the three nurses being briefed were given no encouragement to show any emotion. Sister was in with Ben. Simon ran through the case history with icy efficiency. Ben had been off to a school camp, a distraction to keep him from worrying too much about his brother, and a more normal occupation anyway for a ten-year-old than hospital visiting. He had arrived back complaining of a headache and running a mild fever. His parents had thought he might be going down with measles because he grumbled about the light and said it hurt his eyes. Luckily, because of the question of visiting Sebastian, they'd called Simon in early instead of waiting to see. With Ben's headache worse, his temperature rising sharply and several bouts of vomiting, Simon had decided on a lumbar puncture for safety, and by the time Ben had been brought into the clinic, rigors had started to shake him all over. It was probable that he'd inhaled the infection while swimming in a polluted river.

'Any of you nursed a meningitis before?' Simon asked.

'I have,' Deb Adam said quietly, while Vicky and Clarice shook their heads.

'It's fairly rare nowadays, fortunately. We have to try to reduce the fever—tepid sponging. Streptomycin, of course, and it's already been started. One of you with him constantly, two if necessary, and I do mean constantly. Quarter-hourly records. He's on a nasal drip for fluids. Any questions?'

'Has he gone into coma?' Deb Adam asked.

'Yes. Oh, and I want you three constantly on call, understood? No standing in for anyone else, even if you think you're free. We've got the staff,' Simon said bleakly. He left unsaid the other factor—whether, for all their skill and medicines, they had the power to draw ten-year-old Ben back from the dark world which had closed him in.

'Parents . . . ?' Clarice said tentatively.

'May sit with him at any time, though I'd rather they saw me first. I think they may not be here much.' Simon looked down at the desk in front of him suddenly, fiddling with the pen between his fingers, his face a frowning mask. 'There's Bas to visit, and he mustn't be told anything or given the least clue, so . . . If we have to call them in, if it becomes necessary, I'll deal with it. I think for the moment,' his voice was impersonal, but the pen flipped suddenly out of his grasp to land on the desk with a clatter, 'they've got enough on their plates, and can't face much more. Bear it in mind, if they do come in.'

He knew the Stafford parents well, having treated Sebastian. There was a second's silence, then Simon spoke again.

'One other thing before you go, and it's an important one. Talk to him. Whatever you're doing, from sponging him down to just watching him—talk! That's one of the reasons I chose you three, not just because you're capable, but because you communicate with your patients. Staff Nurse Adam, like to tell us why the talking is necessary?'

'Like any other coma patient, sir? Trying to keep up a brain response?'

'Right. And don't just try—do it! Now, I want all three of you to go in there and look at him. Then two of you stay, with the other one as relief for coffee and meal breaks. Then change over. Now move!'

There began a time which Vicky would look back on as a blur. Ben's room became the centre of her universe. It was touch and go whether he would respond to the streptomycin, for his temperature stayed dangerously high and the small unconscious body seemed to be burning away. The nasal drip which nourished him needed watching when he jerked into sudden spasms of shivering which locked his muscles hard. His lips and mouth needed moistening against their terrible dryness and the tepid sponging, and the careful changing of his bedclothes without moving him too much, seemed almost constant. A portable scanner was brought in and the quiet blip of that made a background to the constant murmur of talk which went on not between the nurses, but to Ben himself as they told him what they were doing, chatted about anything which might interest a ten-year-old, and reminded him of stories one or other of them had heard him reading aloud to Sebastian during a dialysis session.

Simon, looking weary but controlled, was in and out. And if Vicky's heart gave a squeeze at the sight of him, she was too occupied to do more than acknowledge it and carry on with what she was doing. It was more painful when Mr Stafford came in and went away again quickly after trying to say a few words to his son in a voice which broke. He had winced at the sight of the scanner. Vicky had guessed that he had seen too much machinery attached to his sons.

She supposed the rest of the clinic was functioning normally—in fact she knew it must be. Every time she emerged from Ben's room some nurse or other would ask her how things were going.

Ben's temperature stabilised, but he remained deeply unconscious. The possibility that he might stay there was something Vicky wouldn't let herself consider and she was aware that Clarice and Deb felt the same. She had scarcely known Deborah before but the three of them had turned into a unit with the ability to catch each other's unspoken thoughts. All of them went off duty unwillingly and came back with deliberate hope. Ben was *alive*. There wouldn't necessarily be permanent brain-damage. He would wake up one of these days.

On the morning when he did, Vicky wasn't in the

room. She had gone down for her coffee-break, Deb coming in to relieve her—then she would go back and relieve Clarice. Vicky was trying not to make an angry answer to the nurse who would insist on reminding everyone gloomily that Ben had been in coma for a solid week now, when the rest-room door burst open. Vicky jerked to her feet and was making for the doorway even as Clarice stumbled through it, because the other girl was in tears. Clarice, who stayed bouncy through almost everything, who was immensely efficient but claimed never to be involved enough with any patient to take her worries home with her. Vicky felt an instant's cold dread. Then the other girl was hugging her, and shrieking,

'He's round. He opened his eyes. He's awake! Si—Simon sent me out of there—told me off for not being d—detached enough—' She gulped, and rubbed at her tearstained cheeks with her hand, adding defiantly, 'But *he* was trying not to grin from ear to ear while he put on that steely voice! And d'you know what our little tyke had just done? He opened his eyes and looked up at me in a kind of puzzled way and then said, "Is it time to get up? Where's Mum?"'

A buzz of pleasure ran all round the room, and someone laughed. Vicky hugged Clarice hard and wondered why she didn't burst into tears herself—she was suddenly aching all over with relief! There would still be a lot of nursing to do for Ben of course, and a battery of tests to see if there were any after-effects, but he had pulled through! She felt like dancing on the ceiling and knew Clarice was feeling the same. Deb would be feeling it too, behind the cool nurse's manner she was so good at keeping up. And Simon, him most of all, because in spite of his cold words to Clarice, Vicky knew that he'd been carrying the heaviest load of all of them over the past days. He had been working tirelessly, constantly on call in spite of all his other patients, keeping in touch with the

Staffords as well as monitoring Ben, grim and terse with all the clinic staff even though he still managed the same calm gentleness as usual with his patients. He had even been sleeping at the clinic, going back to Belville Close only to change his clothes. Ben's night staff who took over at eleven said that Simon was often in to see the boy during the night, on top of his daytime case-load.

He must be tired. Vicky didn't realise how weary she was herself. The intensive hours she had worked seemed to have merged together and she was still caught up in the tension of them. With Ben showing a remarkably rapid improvement now that he was conscious, his speech and reflexes thankfully normal, his intensive care nurses were given three full days off.

But Vicky couldn't settle. She told herself that it was because she wanted to be there seeing Ben improve, becoming daily more like any other convalescent child. She brooded on the fact that Simon was still sleeping at the clinic too, because it gave her the feeling that something was still going on which she didn't know about.

And besides, she missed him. Simon as the doctor, with his passionate involvement in his work—Simon as the man who could make her heart turn over just by walking into a room. All the tangled emotions she had been pushing aside came back to plague her. She found she was mooning around the house in case he came back and resenting it when he didn't.

As a result, when he did come back she almost snapped at him. It was late in the evening of her second day off and she was sitting cross-legged on the sofa watching an exceptionally dull television programme. It was on loud enough for her to have missed hearing Simon's key in the downstairs door. When the tall, familiar figure appeared in the doorway like a sudden apparition, Vicky jumped. It was all she could do not to bite out bad-temperedly, 'So there you are at last!' and it made it somehow worse to see him drawn with tiredness

and with a distinct five-o'clock-shadow staining his jaw.
She tried to answer the pleasant smile he was giving her,
and said sharply,

'How's Ben?'

'Doing fine, I'm glad to say. He's as hungry as a small
horse, and wants to know if he'll be out of hospital
before Bas is because he wants to go and see him in his
anti-infection bubble again.' Simon stretched, and wandered in the direction of his bedroom door, so that Vicky
had to call out after him. Even to her own ears, her voice
sounded faintly accusing.

'Why are you still sleeping at the clinic then, if everything's all right?'

'Just being extra careful. I've given it up now.' He had
gone into his bedroom without taking any further notice
of her, and his voice floated back. 'Paul and Claire
Stafford want to see the three of you personally, by the
way, to thank you. You did a good job. Oh, why is there
a joke going round the clinic that Ben's going to grow up
to be a winger, do you know?'

'C—Clarice told him all the rules of rugby football
that's all, as something which might interest him enough
to wake him up—'

Idiotically, tears were suddenly sliding down Vicky's
cheeks. She didn't know how to stop them and her voice
must have sounded odd too, because Simon was suddenly there at his bedroom door looking at her. She
didn't know whether she was crying because he was
talking to her in such an ordinarily friendly voice, or for
Ben, or for herself, but she couldn't seem to stop. She
gulped hard and said chokily, 'S—sorry . . .'

'You haven't managed to unwind yet, have you?'

'Are you going t—to tell me off for being too
involved?'

'No.' He looked at her for a moment, then he gave her
a suddenly vivid smile. The tall form crossed the room
towards her and when he sat down beside her his arm

went round her shoulders to draw her against him with warm comfort. 'No, so don't smoulder at me. For one thing I'm too tired to quarrel. For another, *I* can't say that. I've grown fond of Ben . . .'

'We're *all* fond of him.'

'Shouldn't make any difference. Doesn't, in a way. When you're fighting for a life, that's what it is—a life. Try to concentrate on the fact that we won, mm? The three of you, especially. It must have been tough keeping up all that chatting. I'm not going to apologise for putting you through it—'

'No, don't!'

'—because I chose you particularly for your capacity to nag!' He sounded almost like the old Simon, though Vicky could feel, as she leaned against him, that he was weary to the bone. No, it wasn't a time to quarrel about anything with him. It was all at once immensely peaceful to be curled up close to him, with the simple pleasure of his nearness soothing the jagged edges of her nerves. Her tears dried and she wanted nothing so much as this feeling of belonging. 'It must have felt like nagging sometimes,' he was going on, tiredness deepening his voice, 'when it's instinctive to let a sick person rest. I wonder if he will remember any of it? We don't know enough about the brain . . . He seems remarkably bright considering all he's been through. Tough little nut, thank goodness. We'll be able to let him go home to convalesce soon.' He turned his head against Vicky's hair, a movement which might simply have been weariness, but still felt like a caress. 'But if you're going to say you'll miss him, don't, or I *will* tell you off! It's another thing that comes with the territory. We patch them up and send them home and concentrate on the next one. And the next. Don't we?'

'Yes, I do know. It just—isn't always easy—'

'I know. It's like walking a tightrope. You care, but you don't let it tear you apart. You can't do the job

properly without seeing each child as a whole person,
but when the pressure's off you have to make yourself let
go. Otherwise we'd all crack up and be no use to
anyone.' Simon stretched a little, so that she felt the
muscles of his chest move against her. 'I don't really
have to tell you all that, do I? You're too good a nurse
not to know it already. Talking of that,' he added, with
the weariness which edged his voice making him sound a
little bleary all of a sudden, 'John Grantly was fidgetting
because you weren't there to take his latest tonsils. I told
him you were having a well-deserved rest, as you should
be! I think he's trying to co-opt you. He was on about
borrowing you for some case somewhere else.'

'Oh dear, must I? I mean,' Vicky said hastily, feeling a
glow because at least Simon had called her a good nurse,
'It's nice of him of course, but . . .'

'You needn't if you don't want to. I've already told
him no, as a matter of fact.' Simon stirred again, and this
time his hand came up to touch Vicky's face, to tilt her
chin up towards him. She found the hazel eyes studying
her with a thoughtfulness which made her heart turn
over, and he was so close that she could feel his breath on
her cheek. He looked at her for a long moment and then
said, 'Feeling better?'

'I'm fine. Sorry.'

'Don't be, it catches everyone sometimes. Now,' he
said, on a tone of apology to match her own and with a
rueful gleam coming into his eyes, 'I simply must get
some sleep. Pity . . .'

'I was just thinking that it was *you* who needed the
well-deserved rest.' Vicky said the words quickly, with a
breathlessness which came from the way he had drawled
that last word so softly. She wriggled away from him
abruptly and stood up, saying brightly so as to show him
that she really was all right, 'Shall I haul you up off the
sofa? I could, you know—I used to be very good at
orthopaedic lifting!'

'I think I can manage to get that far by myself.' He came to his feet to prove it, giving her another odd, thoughtful look as she stepped quickly out of his way. He answered her smile, but there was a palpable weariness about him which had him swaying a little on his feet. After the briefest hesitation he turned away to wander back in the direction of his bedroom. Watching him go, Vicky felt a mixture of regret, longing, and the desire to go after him and tuck him up in bed. She bit her lip, and her hand stole to her face where the long, strong fingers had touched it.

His voice came from somewhere out of sight, as she could hear him moving about his bedroom. 'Vicky, you still there?'

'Yes?'

'You're still off duty all day tomorrow, aren't you?'

'Yes—yes, I am.' Her heart jerked with sudden hope. This time, she wasn't doing anything, and wouldn't invent anything either.

'I've got a long consultation tomorrow—Downs Syndrome baby—and another couple of consultations I had to postpone before. Could you be an angel and take my washing to the laundrette for me?'

'Yes, of course!'

Her answer came out with polite clarity, against the thud of disappointment which caught her under the ribs and the taste of chagrin in her mouth. Yes, of course she'd be useful. That was what housemates were for. She heard him tell her, on a yawn, that he'd leave a plastic bag where she couldn't avoid falling over it, to remind her.

Foolish to imagine that he'd been holding her a moment ago out of anything other than the brotherly concern he'd show to anyone who was upset. Or perhaps what she'd been receiving was the professional gentleness which he showed to his young patients.

Vicky bit her lip again, this time in an anger she knew

was unfair. How could she be angry with him for taking the trouble to be kind to her at a time when he was almost too tired to think straight? It wasn't his fault that she didn't want his kindness. Nor his casual, occasional interest either, but something much more.

She recalled suddenly that the last time he'd told her something 'came with the territory' he was talking about listening to Jennifer Dane's matrimonial problems. As she walked soft-footed up the stairs to her bedroom Vicky reminded herself again that at least he wasn't in love with Jennifer.

She made herself remember the Callenders because it seemed a good way of cheering herself up, instead of yearning over the thought of Simon climbing sleepily into bed downstairs. It had been fun nursing Jimmy. Marc had been nice, too, with his humour and patience and total lack of pretension about being a film star. Considering the circumstances of the Callenders' divorce, it still seemed unfair that Simon had warned her against Marc. With a sudden wry defiance Vicky thought that it was a pity Marc wasn't still around if he was the sort of man who made even Simon bristle a little. Yes, it was definitely a pity that Marc wasn't still visiting the clinic and attracting a lot of notice and smiling his crinkly smile at everyone.

Just under a week later, while she was doing some late shopping after finishing her early evening duty, Vicky bumped into Marc Callender in the middle of Selfridges.

CHAPTER NINE

SHE wouldn't have expected him to remember her. He did, though, with every evidence of pleasure. She asked after Jimmy, and was told that the small boy was completely himself again, as lively as a cricket.

'And you? Are you just coming off duty, or going on to it?' Marc indicated her uniform coat, his eyes alert and interested.

'Coming off.' She had come down to wander round the store with a moody feeling because number ten Belville Close promised to be empty yet again this evening. Since Ben had gone home Simon seemed even busier than ever with a burst of appointments, consultations and conferences which took him all over the place. He had flown to Edinburgh for a one-day symposium, driven to Milton Keynes to give a lecture and been called to Kent for a second opinion. And tonight he was going to a medical dinner at University College Hospital. At least that's where he said he was going, telling her so during breakfast and mentioning casually that he didn't expect to be back late. Since Vicky had only seen him in passing for several days she wondered sourly why he should expect her to want to know. She smiled at Marc now, trying not to feel shy because he was looking at her with that intent blue gaze he always had for whoever he was talking to, and said lightly, 'We're not very busy at the moment, which makes a change!'

'A nice one, I should think.' He slipped a hand under her arm to move her out of the way of a gaggle of passing shoppers, at least one of whom was gazing at him with an intrigued recognition which he ignored. He went on holding on to her in a friendly fashion, still giving her his full attention. 'I'll tell you what—since you obviously haven't had a heavy day, why don't you come out and have dinner with me?'

Vicky blinked at him, startled. She was used to his friendliness while she was nursing Jimmy, but—her? Go out to dinner with someone as famous as Marc Callender? She saw his eyebrows go up quizzically at her expression and found herself stammering, 'That's very . . . But aren't you . . . ?'

'I'm sure I owe you a dinner for looking after Jimmy so well. Or have you got a heavy boyfriend who's going to come round and beat me up for asking?'

'No. No, I certainly haven't.'

'Well then. We can always talk about Jimmy, and how he's settling down to the idea of having a stepfather as well as a visiting papa.' Marc pulled a face at her suddenly, his skin crinkling up into its familiar laughter lines. 'I said that in case you don't happen to read the papers and were worrying about the fact that I was a married man—were you?'

'No, actually, I do read the papers.' It was remarkably easy to relax with him and to respond to his charm. All the same Vicky asked, hesitantly, 'Is Jimmy happy?'

'Oh, he's fine. He likes Laurence. The whole thing's very friendly. As much my fault as Jennifer's,' Marc said deprecatingly. 'I'm always away so much. I'll still see Jim as much as ever and he isn't going to be in the middle of a lot of quarrels. Less than there used to be, in fact.' There was a serious touch in his voice for once, and Vicky liked him for it. He didn't seem to mind that he was standing in the middle of Selfridges discussing his divorce with a half-stranger, either. It occurred to Vicky that he was probably so used to carrying on his life in a blaze of publicity that he didn't even notice it. He certainly didn't seem to notice how many people stared at him and then started whispering excitedly to each other, though it gave *her* a strange feeling of unreality. She found that

Marc was giving her his pleasant smile and watching her with cheerful enquiry. 'You'll have dinner with me, then? And cheer my—um—current bachelorhood?'

'I'd like to very much. Thank you. I'll have to go home and change,' Vicky told him, feeling a suddenly renewed shyness at the unexpectedness of the whole thing and looking up at him uncertainly. She didn't have to look very far up because he really was quite short for a man—or perhaps it was just that she was used to Simon, she thought suddenly.

'Yes of course. Give me the address and I'll come and pick you up—about eight? Good. I'll look forward to that, Vicky!'

Going home on the bus, Vicky was still feeling unreal. Dinner with Marc Callender no less! It was funny, but when she was actually with him it was the easiest thing in the world to feel as if she knew him quite well—and after all she had spent quite a lot of time in his company when she was nursing Jimmy. She still thought of him as a likeable man rather than a glamorous one, though she was aware of his charm. She started wondering what to wear, riffling rapidly through the contents of her wardrobe in her mind, disconcerted by the fact that she didn't know what sort of place he was likely to take her to. Then, with an abruptness which was almost like plotting, she found herself hoping that Simon would be at home and changing to go out at the same time as she was. He would probably ask her, in that pleasantly civil manner of his, where she was going, and she would tell him.

Unfortunately he wasn't there. Vicky dressed carefully in the outfit she had chosen, a swirling full skirt and a matching off-the-shoulder top with a deep frill round it in a dark red cotton so finely woven that it was as soft as wool. She had bought it on impulse and hadn't worn it before tonight, but she knew it suited her. It was also something which could look as formal or informal as the surroundings required. The evenings were darkening earlier now that the chill of autumn was in the air, but she could team up the outfit with a cream fringed shawl covered with embroidered flowers in different colours. She brushed her hair hard until it stood out in a wild halo round her head, the length still falling softly beyond her shoulders, and did her make-up with extra care. Looking at herself critically in the mirror, she couldn't help knowing that the whole effect was good. In fact, it was a triumph to realise suddenly that even Marina would have had to compete. And Marina, with her striking auburn hair, couldn't have worn this colour red.

Simon still wasn't there to notice her, which gave Vicky a pang of annoyance as she went downstairs to wait for Marc to arrive. A pang of wistfulness too. She was guiltily aware that she should have been dressing up so carefully because she was going out with the famous Marc Callender, not because she wanted to be seen by Simon. Second thoughts told her that Marc could undoubtedly look after himself, so she didn't have to feel guilty about him when he probably wouldn't particularly have cared what she was looking like for a dinner-date he had handed out merely on a casual impulse. In fact he might even have changed his mind and wouldn't come. She shouldn't really count on it, and she realised with a sudden uncertainty that she didn't really want to count on it, either. What was she doing in this unlikely situation?

Marc arrived to pick her up on the dot of eight in an open MG sports car which was one of the kind which had become collector's pieces. Seeing him there on the doorstep, with a wide smile of approval for her appearance and an admiring if humorous look in his bright blue eyes, made Vicky feel uncertain all over again. As he ushered her into the car he apologised solicitously for the fact that she might get blown about a bit and she assured him that it didn't matter. When he gave another glintingly amused but admiring look at her hair and said no, he supposed it didn't and wasn't that lucky, she found herself laughing. He really was an amazingly easy person to be with. Perhaps it was just that there were so many things about him that reminded her of Jimmy, but she relaxed into his company in no time at all. She didn't even notice it much when the casually smart restaurant he took her to made an especial point of shifting someone else's reservation around to give them the table Marc preferred.

They sat in a booth which was almost like a horse's stall only rather more elegant. They talked at first about what it was like filming—boring, Marc said, and he often thought he'd been doing it too long. The trouble was, he wasn't trained to do anything else but act so he was stuck with doing just that. He seemed perfectly cheerful about it. Vicky refused to talk to him about nursing because that, she told him lightly, really would bore him—at which he gave her a mischievous grin and agreed. They were half way through steak served with some delicious and elaborate sauce when he smiled his crinkly smile at her and said casually,

'Shall we have an affair?'

Vicky's fork was abruptly suspended half way to her mouth. It was lucky she didn't have a mouthful, or she might have choked. Instead she found herself saying,

'Sorry—what?'

'I said, shall we have an affair? Why not?'

He didn't seem to be teasing. Looking at him, at the square pleasant face, the dark hair, the apparently innocent blue eyes, Vicky was so much reminded of Jimmy asking if he could have some more ice cream that she couldn't take the question at all seriously. She found herself asking with curiosity,

'Are you always as direct as that?'

'Oh yes. It's much the easiest way and it saves an awful lot of time. Then we both know where we stand, don't we?' He gave her a caressing look, though he didn't

make any attempt to touch her. 'I can't resist beautiful
girls, and you really are beautiful. That was most of the
trouble between me and Jennifer—my low powers of
resistance. You see, I'm quite honest about it!'

He wasn't even bothering to look penitent. Vicky
stared at him. This was a different Marc Callénder from
the one she knew, but actually it was impossible to be
cross with him. He decided he wanted something, so he
asked for it—and usually got it, she supposed. She felt a
sudden sympathy for Jennifer, but Marc was saying
amiably, and without losing any of his air of mischievous
good-humour, 'You haven't answered. You can say yes,
no, or maybe.'

'No—thank you!'

'Oh dear, that was a bit prompt. I thought I might at
least get a maybe.'

'You make it sound like snakes and ladders,' Vicky
said drily. Marc, rather to her surprise, found the comment extremely funny and started to laugh.

'Oh, you'd be good for me, Vicky, you really would!
We might even be good for each other. We come from
such different worlds. Don't you think it would be fun?
After all, if you're not in love with anyone else at the
moment—'

'I am,' Vicky said involuntarily. Suddenly the evening
was spoiled, not because of Marc's open overtures,
which had been flattering, she supposed, in their way—
but because she wanted to go home and see Simon and
feel at least the comfort of his presence even when that
presence made her feel moody and frustrated. She cast a
swift, embarrassed glance at Marc, seeing him as a
stranger rather than the easy and attentive companion of
the earlier part of the evening. 'Sorry,' she muttered, 'I
didn't mean to—It isn't—'

'It isn't going well, obviously, from the look on your
face.' Marc, to her even greater surprise, sounded
genuinely sympathetic. 'What's the trouble? Is he tied

up with somebody else?'

'No . . . Look, I'm sorry,' Vicky said miserably, putting both her knife and her fork down and gazing at him with a mixture of guilt and unhappiness. I'll—I'll go—'

'No, finish your meal, silly girl. I'll stop propositioning you if things are *that* way, so don't worry. You can even tell me all about it,' Marc said, with absolutely no sign of being offended, 'and I'll talk to you like a Dutch uncle. Which will be good practice for later when I'm having to take older parts, won't it?'

There was a flash of that endearing, uncomplicatedly mischievous smile again, and that same look of innocent collusion. Vicky, gazing at him with some of her embarrassment still with her, wondered how he could manage to be so likeable and so—amoral, she supposed—at the same time. He seemed to see life in entirely practical terms, and she certainly couldn't imagine anyone else she had ever met reacting as he did.

She didn't mean to say anything else at all about her problems, but then found him drawing the information out of her with a light, friendly sympathy. She left out names, of course, and anything about the situation which would give him a clue as to the identity of the main party. There was just a man whose house she happened to be living in, who happened to have been in love with her sister. She tried to make the situation sound laughable, but he gave it his serious attention—true, not without crinkling up into mischief once or twice, but without ever making him feel he was laughing at her. He seemed capable of taking a genuine interest in other people's lives, but when she commented on that with a touch of shyness, he raised his eyebrows and said, why not? Plays and films were made up out of people's lives. And then, rather to her relief, they went on to talk about plays and films, and he was thoroughly amusing about some of the parts he had played.

The evening might not have turned out in a way that either of them could have expected, but it had lightened back into friendliness. They sat a long time over coffee with Marc being charming, a little cynical, and apparently as interested in Vicky's views as in his own. While he was signing for the bill, she thought with a renewed self-consciousness that for all his ability not to show it, he was probably glad the evening was over. Then she found it wasn't. Marc said,

'Come on—let's go dancing. I know a night-club where we're likely to meet up with some friends of mine. You'll like them, or at least you'll find them interesting!'

'Wouldn't you rather—'

'Not unless you're offering to turn that no to yes—and you're not, are you?' Marc gave her a frank, amused look, and shook his head in mock sadness. He picked up her shawl to put it round her shoulders with an automatic attentiveness, letting his fingers trail down her arms in a light caress. 'No, pretty Vicky, I'll tell you what you're going to do. You're going to go home very late and bang about like a burglar until that man of yours gets up to see what's happening. Then you can drape yourself round the furniture looking sexy and telling him what a marvellous night you've had without him. If he doesn't go mad with jealousy—if he *still* can't stop thinking about your sister—then give him up, because he's obviously cold-blooded! There you are, them's the fruits of my wisdom!'

He was laughing, or he might have noticed Vicky's slight guilty jump. It was almost as if he had read her earlier thoughts about making Simon jealous. She decided abruptly that she would go dancing with Marc anyway because he was good company, immensely kind in his own light-hearted way, and besides, it would be an experience to retail to Clarice. If to no one else. She climbed into Marc's car with determined gaiety, and even felt a mild thrill when a passing group of people paused to stare at her enviously.

The night-club was dim, smoky, full of disco music, flashing lights, and a lot of smart people. Marc seemed to be well-known there. He danced with her at first and then they were drawn into a crowd. Vicky recognised several faces she'd only seen in magazines before, but they all seemed to accept her as one of themselves. A busty blonde who Vicky was sure she'd seen in a television sitcom wound herself around Marc, and Vicky found herself with a tall, cadaverous young man who gazed at her in total silence, then closed his eyes and danced in a trance-like state without ever bumping into anyone. She saw a stage actor, as well-known as Marc, looking scruffily unshaven in jeans and a torn shirt and arguing fiercely with someone about something. There seemed to be a lot of very young, very beautiful girls about and quite a number of middle-aged men. Everyone was either very animated, or very cool.

It was a little while before Vicky noticed a couple sniffing something from tiny silver spoons which they wore on chains round their necks—and she immediately wished she hadn't seen them. She washed up against Marc a little while later, and stood with him among the crowd—but when the group began to break up, and a thin-faced forty-ish man on the fringes of it started eyeing her with obvious intent, she caught at Marc's arm.

'Hey—'she smiled at him apologetically. 'Would you mind if I went home? I've got to work tomorrow!'

'Poor busy little nurse!' He said it lightly, with his charming smile, but he reached over to retrieve her shawl for her from the back of a chair. 'Would *you* mind,' he said in her ear, with an arm round her to thread her through the crowd towards the door, 'if I put you in a taxi? I've got hopes of a certain blonde, who's got as far as *maybe*—'

Vicky turned her head to see his wicked grin. 'Of

course I don't mind,' she told him, unable to prevent herself grinning back at him. There really wasn't any need to wish him good luck, she thought with genuine amusement. She still couldn't help liking him, though she hadn't altogether liked his friends, particularly not the ones with the wandering hands. She didn't say so, of course, but gave a little shiver as Marc took her out into the night air, snaffled a taxi with expert speed and gave her a swift, comprehensive kiss while she was in the middle of thanking him for the evening. The kiss was pleasant, but didn't do anything to her at all.

He had paid the driver and all she had to do was sit back in it and review the evening. It had been a strange experience, a mixture of fun and disillusionment. She didn't think she'd like to belong in Marc's cynical, casual world—in fact she was sure she wouldn't, and she wrinkled her nose a little at the knowledge that the night-club had given her a sense of danger. He had seemed to fit in a little too well there, too. She had liked him better on the whole as Jimmy's father. He was a very accomplished charmer, she could see that now, though there was also a side of him which was very pleasant, friendly, and sympathetic. She was trying not to think about getting back to Belville Close and about Marc's advice to bang about like a burglar, so when the taxi pulled up she was jerked back into the present with a quiver of uncertainty. She didn't have to follow his advice, of course. A glance at her watch as the taxi drove away showed her that it wasn't actually as late as it felt. Only one o'clock. The curtained windows of the house seemed to mock at her. Simon might not be in himself, of course.

But there was a dim line of light under the sitting-room door as she let herself into the house. Well, he was in, then. And still up. He might have brought a medical colleague back with him from the dinner and be sitting their talking shop. Vicky bit her lip, aware that her pulse was bumping unevenly as she went lightly up the stairs. A nervous giggle really wasn't the effect she wanted . . . She took a deep breath and went through the door quickly with a swirl of her skirts.

Simon was sitting in one of the armchairs with only a low table-lamp for company, bathing him in a pool of light in the shadowy room. He was in full evening dress and although he had loosened the collar and left the tie hanging undone, the black and white set off his handsomeness with an elegance which made Vicky's breath catch in her throat. A magazine on the chair-arm beside him showed that he had been sitting up reading, but he must have heard Vicky coming, because he wasn't reading now. She met a dark, level gaze which took in her heightened colour, the wild aureole of her hair, the bare shoulders where her shawl had slipped down away from them. She knew that there must be a nervous sparkle in her eyes which she hoped he would take as vivacity, or surprise at seeing him and she rushed into bright speech.

'Oh, hallo, are you still up? I wasn't expecting to see you.'

'Yes, I am. I've been sitting here wondering when you'd get in.' He bit out the words with such a suppressed anger that Vicky almost flinched, but it was so much the reaction she wanted from him that her heart gave a wild jump. She opened her mouth to make some light, airy answer—if she could only find enough breath—but he added abruptly, searingly, 'Or *if* you were going to get in, of course!'

'Goodness, you haven't really been sitting up for me, have you? Why on earth should you do that?' There, that was better, and if her voice sounded uneven and a little high, perhaps he wouldn't notice. She added, 'As a matter of fact I've been out with—'

'Yes, I know who you've been out with! Chris just happened to tell me who she'd seen picking you up, when I dropped in over there! Marc Callender really is very recognizable, you know!' Sarcasm and anger mingled in his voice. 'That's who you've been spending so much time with lately, is it? Even if it's the first time he's turned up openly? I suppose we should be glad you've spared the time to come to work!'

'That's an unfair comment if ever I heard one!' Vicky retorted angrily, genuinely stung. She caught herself up on it quickly, and made herself step closer into the pool of light with a movement which she hoped would look casual. 'What's wrong with Marc, anyway?' she said airily. 'He's not married any more—at least he's definitely separated, isn't he, when his wife's already announced that she's going to marry someone else—so if he wants to take me out—And I hadn't realised, anyway, that you were *policing* me! Anyone would think—'

'Anyone would think you were an empty-headed little chit instead of a reasonably intelligent nurse!' Simon came to his feet abruptly, his magazine flying off the chair-arm with the violence of his movement, his height towering over Vicky in a way which made her suddenly want to retreat behind something. He was in more of a rage than she had bargained for . . . She thought for a second that he was going to catch hold of her and shake her, but he turned away to take two paces across the room. Over his shoulder he grated, 'But if you can let a man like that make love to you—'

'He hasn't.'

'Then he's being unusually slow off the mark—if you 'll forgive the pun!' Simon had swung round to glare at her scornfully. 'If you're really too blind to see for yourself what sort of a person he is, you might at least have the sense to listen when someone warns you! But I suppose you couldn't resist—' He bit the words off, his face dark with anger and scorn, the tension in his jaw giving his mouth a bitter twist. 'I suppose it didn't occur to you, either, that I don't hand out warnings without good reason? Or that, since I brought you to London,

I'm responsible for you?'

Not jealousy at all, nothing so personal as that. Vicky's hope solidified into cold stone—but anger came sweeping in to fill the sudden desolate emptiness inside her. 'Oh, it's *responsibility* that makes you carry on like that, is it?' she spat at him, her voice shaking with a sudden fury as great as his own. 'Who to—my sister? Is it because of her that I'm not allowed to choose my own friends? Well, big deal, but I rather think she's been too busy to think about appointing you as my guardian! Besides, I don't actually need one, *thanks*—'

'Don't you? You're certainly too much of a little innocent to mix with Marc Callender's crowd!'

'Then the sooner I stop being a little innocent the better! I happen to be fully grown up! And what do you know about me, anyway? You've—you've invented an identity for me ever since I arrived!' She was so angry that she took a step towards him, her fists clenching with the desire to hit out at him physically. To touch him . . . She was shaking all over, fury mingling with a longing she wouldn't admit. 'I've only been out with Marc once so far, but if he asks me again I'll certainly go! And it'll take more than your—your *disinterested* sense of responsibility to stop me!'

Simon had lunged for her. His hands were on her bare shoulders with a roughness which bruised them. As he caught her to him Vicky was so much in the grip of her rage that she lashed out at him, though he was so much taller and stronger that she couldn't do anything but beat ineffectually against his shoulders. She gasped out, 'Don't take your temper out on *me*!' but she was suddenly weak all over, the shuddering deep in her stomach coming from desire more than anger, the heat of his body against hers bringing every nerve-cell fizzing into life so that currents seemed to course through her blood. Somehow the two of them had collapsed in a tangled heap on the sofa and her arms had flown up round his

neck and his face was coming down on hers in a kiss of
such bruising passion that everything was drowned except pleasure. There was only the warmth of him, the
hard-muscled body holding her close, and closer still,
the taste of his mouth as his lips forced hers apart to draw
all of herself out into a fierce mingling . . .

She found that she was breathing again. That someone else's breath was fanning her face raggedly from an
inch away. That the pounding in her ears was still there
but could be identified as a heartbeat—his, beating as
much of a tattoo as hers. Her eyes fluttered open, to look
into the intense gleam of dark irises above her. Her
breasts were tingling against the heavy thump of his
heart, but the hard tension of his arms moved a little, as
if with deliberate effort, releasing her fractionally. He
said, very softly, breathlessly, on an uneven note which
held a touch of grimness in it,

'You'd better move away if you don't want to get more
than you bargained for.'

The shrill ring of the phone cut across the room, the
noise sending a flash of shock through both of them so
that Vicky's fingers tightened involuntarily in Simon's
hair where they seemed, somehow, to be buried. Simon
didn't seem to notice. His eyes narrowed in annoyance
and he said, 'Oh *God*,' on a note of sheer, unmixed
frustration—but he was disentangling himself even as he
said it. His movement away made Vicky feel as if parts of
her were being torn away too, and she watched him as
he crossed the room with a feeling of dizziness—the
tall, lean darkness of him, the tumbled elegance of his
evening jacket, the hard strength of his jaw.

'Yes? Yes, this *is* Simon Harraday. What?' His voice
was deep and curt, with a frown in it which was already
there on his face, and increased as he listened. 'Is he
there now? No? But he wanted me to—Look, I'd better
come. Yes, I said I'll come. I'll be there in about five
minutes.'

The phone went down on to its rest. Simon turned to look at Vicky. There was enough in the look to send heat coursing through her again, though he didn't take even one step in her direction. He said levelly,

'We have some unfinished business, and you needn't think I'm going to forget it! Now, I've got to go out!'

He went, pausing only long enough to fling off his dress coat and replace it with another one. Vicky was still in a dazed heap on the sofa when she heard the front door bang behind him, and she went on sitting there for several minutes. Part of her mind and all of her body was glowing. She didn't care about Marina. She didn't care about anything, just as long as Simon didn't forget about that unfinished business. She wondered when he would come back.

She fell asleep listening for him. She hadn't set the alarm because she wasn't due to work until one, but she woke early just the same, with her memory flooding back at once and a quiver as she wondered whether Simon was in the house. She was in her bra and pants when she heard the doorbell ring downstairs in a long peal, and when it rang again almost at once, realised that it must be Simon out there and that he had gone out in such a hurry that he'd forgotten his key. She couldn't just leave him standing out there while she dressed. She bit her lip and wrapped her thin nylon dressing-gown round herself with hasty fingers, telling herself shakily not to be silly, because he had seen her in all sorts of situations, busy and tired and cross and weepy and downright *plain*, and at least her hair was looking all right because she'd just brushed it. Then she ran downstairs on bare feet to open the door.

She found herself staring at curly fair hair, a chunky, square-shouldered figure, and a face which ought to have seemed totally familiar, but was so out of place that she blinked as if at a stranger.

'*Andrew?*'

'Vicky?' he said on the same note of disbelief. 'I'd scarcely have recognised you. But it is you, isn't it?' He gave her a distracted look which wasn't altogether approving. 'Look, I'm sorry about this, but can I come in?'

'Er—yes, of course. Is—is Marina with you?'

'No, she's not,' he said shortly. He edged round Vicky as she held the door open for him and he seemed to be peering around as if looking for something. 'What I wondered was . . . As a matter of fact I don't know where she is. Have you—is she here?'

'No.' The monosyllable came out swiftly and flatly. Marina must have told Andrew about living with Simon so presumably his first thought was to come here looking for her. 'You'd better come up,' Vicky said abruptly, and then, catching the dubious look on Andrew's face, 'to the sitting-room! It's on the first floor. This way.'

'Funny way to arrange things.' He said it as if he was trying to make conversation, sounding strained—but Vicky felt impatient with him all the same. Any minute now he'd give her another embarrassed look and tell her to go away and get dressed! Well, he could just put up with her as she was. He was her brother now, after all. As she thought it, she realised abruptly that seeing him had made her think nothing but that—her brother-in-law. She saw that Simon's bedroom door was half-open just as he had left it last night, so he hadn't come back yet. And all at once she wanted to get rid of Andrew quickly rather than have Simon come back and enter into a discussion of where Marina might be. She knew, guiltily, that she ought to be feeling more sympathetic than that, and turned to face Andrew with an attempt at a friendly smile.

'Now then. Marina certainly isn't here. What happened? Did you quarrel, or something?'

'Yes.' Andrew seemed faintly disconcerted by her

brisk tone. Perhaps she'd never spoken to him in her nurse's voice before. Vicky felt guilty all over again as she saw the strain on his face, the outright misery in his eyes. He was gazing at her like a man whose last hope had gone, and also with that faintly bemused, slightly disapproving look he'd given her on the doorstep. 'You've changed,' he said, as if involuntarily.

'Yes, probably. I mean—yes, one does. D'you want to tell me about it? About what's happened between you and Marina, I mean? You don't have to, but if it would help—'

'Not really. She's left me.' He sounded more aggrieved about it than anything else, though there was still that lost look in his eyes. 'I thought she might have come to you. Well, you are her sister, after all, and I don't know who else she knows in London. Lots of people, I suppose. But as it's a family matter I thought she might have come to you. So I rang your mother and pretended I was coming to London for something and asked for your address. It's a sort of lodging house, is it?'

Vicky stifled a slight choke, and covered it with a nod which might have meant anything. Andrew seemed remarkably innocent about the standard of decoration in lodging-houses—she had seen some during her brief hunt for a room. She was adding up swiftly, too, that Marina hadn't told him about living here with Simon. It wasn't that which had brought him at all. 'I haven't seen Marina since the wedding,' she said quietly as she saw him wince. '*Honestly*. And I'm sure she can't have left you for good. Maybe she's just gone off somewhere to think! She's always had a bit of a temper, you know! When did she actually go?'

'Yesterday morning. I came in from Bottom Acre where we'd been fence-mending and she'd gone. She took a suitcase.' Andrew ran a hand distractedly through his hair, and burst out, 'I wish she had come to you!

You're always so sensible—you'd have backed me up about this job thing!'

'Oh. The partnership with Daddy? You didn't want her to take it?'

'No, it wasn't that, she doesn't want to be a GP. A job at the hospital. It would have meant all sorts of hours and we'd hardly have seen each other! Besides, she doesn't have to work. It's a full time job being a farmer's wife,' Andrew said aggrievedly, apparently unaware that the two statements contradicted each other. 'I've told her that. You would have told her that, wouldn't you?'

'I wouldn't, actually, when she's a trained doctor. She'd have earned enough for you to have help in the house, I expect,' Vicky pointed out into Andrew's surprised face, 'and it's *her* job. It's what she does best. Couldn't you think of it like that?'

'*She* didn't, when she agreed to marry me. It's funny,' Andrew said sulkily, 'on the way up here I was thinking that I really should have married *you*, because you understand what farming's all about. I wouldn't have expected to hear you say—'

'We never really knew each other all that well.' Vicky cut him off rapidly, with a feeling of unreality, and even with a touch of anger. 'Marina and I are both doctor's daughters, remember? We can't help how we feel about medicine. And really, Andrew—'

She saw the lost look in his eyes again and it brought her sympathy back, even while she felt exasperated with him. 'Marina loves you,' she said gently, 'I know she does, or she wouldn't have married you. And you love her. You may have had a row about whether or not she takes a job, but it won't last forever. She might even be back home now. I don't know why you thought she'd come to London.'

'It's where she said she'd go if I wouldn't be reasonable. And I do love her,' Andrew said huskily, his pride crumbling suddenly, 'I love her so damn much I don't know how to live without her. She's—she's just every-thing—'

'Then you'll just have to compromise, won't you?' Vicky laid a hand on his arm because he was near tears. 'You can make it work, I know you can. I know you aren't going to let it fall apart at the first problem. You'll just have to talk to each other, quietly and reasonably. If I see her, I'll tell her.'

'Pardon me for interrupting,' a cold deep voice said icily behind her, 'but I'm afraid you'll have to break up this touching scene.'

Vicky had swung round at the first word. Simon's cold stare made his eyes look like dark pin-points. She tum-bled into speech with a sudden startled quake inside her and a foolish, quite irrational pleasure at seeing him which had nothing to do with the way he was glaring at both of them.

'Oh good, you're home.' She felt Andrew stiffen, which reminded her that she still had her hand on his arm. She withdrew it quickly and babbled on. 'You remember Andrew, don't you? He's called in because he's—er—temporarily mislaid Marina. He thinks she came to London, so—'

'Well she certainly isn't here!' Simon addressed the words at a point somewhere above Andrew's head. 'So you'd better look somewhere else for your wife!'

The last word was stressed a fraction too much. When he finished, 'And your wife's sister had better go and get dressed!' the meaning was all too plain. Vicky stared at him wide-eyed. He couldn't really think . . .

She was suddenly aware that Andrew was bristling behind her. Oh lord, the implication had hit him too. She turned to him swiftly, to find him staring at her with an outraged expression on his face, but what he came out with was,

'Vicky, are you living with this man?'

'I do think you'd better go, Andrew! And—and see if Marina's gone back home yet! I'm sure that's the place to wait for her, at the farm, and I'm sure she *will* come home, and you can discuss everything properly. About her taking a job and everything.' The words, with a spark of anger in them, were for Simon as much as for Andrew. 'Give her my love when you see her—and remember what I said about compromising and her work being important to her, and—'

'I really don't want to talk about that in front of a third party,' Andrew said stiffly. He opened his mouth to say something else, but Simon's voice cut across the space between them, coldly.

'Yes, I'm afraid you *had* better go. Sorry to be unsympathetic if you're having trouble with Marina, but it really isn't our business, and we've got work to do. Vicky, I told you to get dressed, and I meant it. And I mean that we've got work to do, too. Hurry up!'

There was no question of arguing with him when he spoke in that voice. He was Dr Harraday at his most steely. Vicky found she was half way up the stairs before she'd even thought about saying goodbye to Andrew, and she went on up them. As she fumbled into her uniform dress with hasty fingers she was still feeling a sparkle of anger, mixed with confusion and doubt and an oddly tremulous certainty. *No*, Simon couldn't still think *that* was going on—that she had any feelings left for Andrew! And if he did she could surely straighten him out in a few words. After last night . . .

She shot down the stairs, fully dressed and pinning her hair up as she went. Work, he'd said. And if that wasn't what he meant . . .

He was waiting for her, still looking unpromisingly grim. She fixed her eyes on those cold dark ones, and said rapidly,

'I'm ready, but if you really meant what I thought you meant just now—'

'We'll have to leave your tendency to pine over your brother-in-law for the moment. There are more important things. We've a patient gone missing. An ex-patient, to be more exact.' He was as terse as if she hadn't been staring at him open-mouthed. 'Her father seemed to think she might have come to us, or more particularly to *you*, at the clinic, and as she's in a disturbed state, we searched the clinic thoroughly just in case. Now I want you to sit down, and think back, and remember everything you can about Charlotte Ryder. A month or so back—Charly, pneumonia. You nursed her. No, don't say a word, just sit still and try to remember *anything*, anything at all, which might give us a clue to where she might have gone!'

CHAPTER TEN

CHARLY. There was no need for Vicky to strain to remember, because the young girl's bony little face came back to her vividly with the name. She concentrated hard to bring back every detail of those two weeks, trying to leave nothing out. They must have thought already of all the obvious things, but she looked up with a swift,

'Her mother?'

'Is in Bermuda. Charly hasn't got her passport with her. Not much money either, not more than a few pounds, her father thinks.'

'The best friend—Camilla something?'

Simon shook his head. 'The Straights haven't seen her. The two girls fell out recently too. I don't know what about, but it seems to have been one of those passionate teenage storms. Camilla certainly hasn't any idea where she is and it sounds as if she's telling the truth.'

'Pop music . . . She listened to it a lot. But then they all do. Discos?'

'Her brothers have been round looking. The police have been informed, and the Salvation Army, since they make a thing out of finding lost teenagers. Father was a bit edgy about the police, but he took my advice.'

'Any pop festivals . . . ? No, I don't think so, as a matter of fact.' She glanced up swiftly at Simon. '*Is* she anorexic?'

'It sounds like it. Father even caught her making herself sick once. He's noticed that she's thinner. That GP of theirs,' Simon said between his teeth, 'is out of contact, as usual.'

'They went to Switzerland, didn't they?'

'Yes, and came back about ten days ago. Charly ran out of the house yesterday morning after a hysterical burst of temper. She'd talked about the clinic quite a lot, and about *you* particularly, saying that you were nice to her. I've gone through all her notes, including the ones you wrote up. There doesn't seem to be anything there to give us a lead.' Simon let out a sigh of exasperation. 'She was moody, she wasn't eating, she was flying into tempers and having crying jags. Driving her father to his wits' end, in fact. There are two older brothers, by the way, and two younger ones—she's the only girl. Custody of the youngest three is going to cause a fight, apparently, so it's hardly surprising if Charly's producing a classic picture of disturbance! But she's on the loose and she really needs to be found immediately, she needs help. Can you think of *anything* . . . ?'

'No,' Vicky said unhappily. 'No, there isn't anything. Places where she used to live as a child? I suppose they've thought. She was trying to go backwards, I think. Oh, and—and I think she may be afraid of the dark. That's all!'

'Okay. It was just on the offchance.'

'Wait a minute!' Vicky took herself back to the small clinic room, the feverish teenager. 'When she was delirious—you remember, when she was first brought in? I had to try to stop her talking, because her breathing was so bad. She kept on about something called How Wood? Hall Wood? She wanted to go there.'

'Let's see if it means anything to her father.' Simon made for the phone and dialled a number swiftly. A few moments' rapid conversation made him swing round to Vicky with, 'Could it have been *Hale* Wood?'

'Yes! Yes, it could easily have been that!' Vicky grasped for memory, and added quickly, 'Rubbing something? Sorry, does that fit in anywhere?'

Simon had gone back to his conversation. Vicky heard

him say, 'About thirty miles out of London? Is it? Yes, I see.' He listened again for a few moments, and scribbled something on the pad beside the phone. Then he said, 'No, you stay there. She might simply come home. Try ringing the Hale Wood number just in case the manor isn't shut up. I'll drive down there. I'll take my nurse with me—yes, the one Charly liked so much. I'll ring back to you when we're there, all right?'

His voice had been practical, with a doctor's calmness, though he was frowning as he swung back to Vicky. 'Hale Wood Manor, with a riding stable attached,' he told her. 'Charly used to go there a lot when she was nine or ten. She was mad about ponies at that stage, and when she wasn't riding she was hanging around there helping. She was staying with cousins nearby—family holiday. The cousins have moved now, and the riding stables closed down, Ryder thinks, a year or two ago. He remembers reading somewhere that the Manor was either standing empty or sold—the name caught his eye because of the family memories of the place. They were all very happy that year. It was when Rufus, the youngest, was born. Worth a try, I think, don't you— since Charly talked about it? A slim chance, but at least we can try and find out if she's been seen in the district!'

'Anything's worth a try.' All this news had brought back Vicky's worries about the child, the worries she had made herself cast off to go on with her job. She had all too clear a memory now, particularly of the frail, bony look the young girl had had. That must be worse now if her father said she was thinner. Besides, anything could happen to a fourteen-year-old girl wandering about alone in a disturbed state. She came to her feet quickly, saying, 'Are we going there now?'

'Yes. I can shelve everything else and leave David to cope with the clinic.' Simon hesitated for a moment, then said, 'No, you're better in uniform, since that's how she's always seen you—that's if we should find her.' He paused again briefly. 'She wouldn't be likely to have *this* address, would she? No, unlikely. I'm ex-directory. We'll go to the clinic first and I'll have to get David to swop cars with me.'

'Oh . . . ?'

'His is larger, in case we find ourselves bringing her back. One can only hope.'

Three-quarters of an hour later they were on the road in Dr Asscher's Citroen, heading southwards out of London amongst the morning traffic. The Citroen might not be as powerful as Simon's Porsche, but it had a back seat onto which he had flung a couple of blankets. He had handed Vicky his scribbled directions, telling her curtly that she could navigate when they reached the right area. Watching him as he drove silently, his face set in a mask, Vicky remembered what else had happened this morning and thought of raising the subject. Then she put the thought aside. Not now, later. There was Charly to think of at the moment. Simon might be treating her in his most coldly impersonal fashion, but he could be like that anyway when there was a crisis involving a patient. When she did speak, it was only to ask suddenly,

'Would she hitch-hike?'

He drew in to the next filling station they came to by way of answer and leaned out to make brief enquiries. They went more slowly after that, keeping an eye out for anyone who might be thumbing at the side of the road. At another filling station, Simon answered Vicky's thought before she had uttered it, saying briefly, 'No photograph—she's taken all the recent ones and torn them up.' As they headed on out of London, he stopped at a couple of lorry parks with their cafés attached, but came back with no comment. At the second, though, he brought her out a cardboard mug of coffee and a sticky bun, handing them to her silently. It was somehow like him to remember that she would have had no breakfast, and she wondered at once whether *he* had. His expression didn't encourage her to ask.

She was resenting his silence a little by the time they were out in the Kent countryside, trying to find Hale Wood Manor amongst the lanes. Vicky was wondering too, with a sudden lowering of spirit, whether being reminded of Marina had upset him. Marina and Andrew *would* have to have quarrelled just now . . . At that moment Simon snapped at her for misreading his scribbled directions and getting them temporarily lost, and that made her concentrate quickly on the job in hand.

Hale Wood Manor, when they found it, was a large house up a long drive with an empty, semi-tended garden. The house was very definitely shut up, though it looked well-kept. The stonework was in good condition and it had recently been painted. There were curtains across all the downstairs windows giving it a blank, shuttered look, but it had the air of a house whose owners were away rather than simply being empty. Simon tried ringing the bell to see if there was a caretaker but there was no reply. No one seemed to be around to ask them who they were or to give them permission for their search, so they decided to investigate further. The stable block, in less good condition than the house and with an overgrown yard in the middle of it, was empty too, and thoroughly locked up. They went all round it trying every door, all the same, and calling Charly's name.

It was chilly, with a lowering autumn greyness. Vicky found herself hoping that wherever Charly was, it was somewhere warm, as a cold wind bit through her cotton dress and uniform coat. By the time they had gone all round the stables, the garden, and walked round the house checking that there wasn't any way into it, she was shivering. She reminded herself that Charly was a lot thinner than she was and had recently had pneumonia too.

'Nothing here, agreed? We'll try the cousins' house now—whoever lives there nowadays.' Yes, Vicky thought obediently, trailing after him as he strode back to the car without waiting for her. But couldn't you say it *nicely*?

They tried the cousins' house. There was a new family in it whose young mother was instantly sympathetic, offered them tea, let Simon use the phone, and said that of course she'd look out for Charly. They toured the lanes. They saw the local police. They tried a nearby village store, bus stops, the nearest railway station several miles away. There seemed to be a lead for a moment when a motor mechanic said he'd seen a young girl climbing a gate in one of the fields, but he was almost sure it was a gipsy child and described her as being roundfaced. Charly still hadn't turned up at home, Simon's phone calls informed them. A sleazy transport café back on the main road hadn't seen a girl of Charly's description either, though Vicky wasn't at all sure the proprietor would have told them if he had. He seemed to think Simon was either a crook or a plain-clothes policeman.

They were back in the nearest village to the manor, with late afternoon closing down around them, when Simon said moodily, 'We've tried everything! We're probably looking in the wrong place, even if there isn't any hard evidence that she's ever tried drugs.'

Vicky knew what he was thinking. If they were wrong, and Charly's disturbance was drug-related, the place to look for her was the inner city. She knew what he must be trying not to think, too; that a man might have picked Charly up and not let her go again, and the violence which could be drawn to young girls. That, and the fact that if Charly went on hiding from the people who cared about her, she could starve herself to death. He sighed sharply.

'We'd better go back, then.'

'Could we go to the manor stables once more? Please?'

'It's getting dark.' He gave her a brief, cool glance with the words.

'Yes, I know, and I think she's afraid of the dark!'

'All right. I hope David's got a torch in his car.'

He had two, one very powerful flashlight and one smaller one. As they drove back up the manor drive Vicky knew that it was probably hopeless, but she couldn't quite leave the place. It nagged her. It was only hope and her own stubbornness, but she had the childish feeling that if she wished hard enough, Charly would be there. Simon drove right up to the stable block this time, passing the dim shadow of the house with the barest glance, and when he parked he left the headlights on so that they shone into the overgrown yard.

'What d'you want to do—go right round all the doors again?'

'I suppose so.'

She looked round at them all, knowing they had rattled all those stable doors once, had pushed at the walls of the barn to see if there were any loose boards and tried every handle. There weren't any broken windows—the owners had at least kept up the stable block to that extent. She walked uncertainly forward, trying to convince herself that she could feel if Charly was there somewhere. An overhanging shadow caught her eye and she hurried quickly forward, telling herself that one stable door hadn't looked quite like that before . . . or perhaps it was only the change of light. It certainly didn't move as she gave it a frustrated rattle. She leaned against it tiredly, watching Simon as he strode along the row opposite shining the flashlight onto every lock and window.

A tiny whimpering sound, just like a sob, came from behind the door she was leaning against.

'*Charly?* Charly, are you in there? It's Vicky—do you

remember, Vicky who nursed you at the clinic?'

The sob came again, more distinctly. Simon was beside her as she pressed her ear against the door, but she ignored his exclamation as she went on speaking.

'Can you open the door, honey? I can't seem to do it from this side. We've got a light out here but I'm not very good with stable doors.'

There was a scrabbling sound, then the feeling of someone moving on the other side. A bolt slid back. Vicky said, with a steadiness she was far from feeling, 'Come on, then, love, I'm freezing out here, and I should think you must be, too! It *is* you, isn't it? I do hope so!'

It was. As the door swung inwards there was the glimpse of a dirty, bony little face as Charly came out into the light and into Vicky's arms, like a terrified child making for shelter. She was shaking and gulping, with that whimpering sound Vicky had first heard, and she was so thin that it was like holding a skeleton.

'It's all right, honey, it's all right. Truly, everything's all right. Come on now. You're quite safe.' Vicky crooned the words with an automatic soothing sound, holding the girl against her, putting on her most placid and practical voice as she said, 'I don't know how you got in there, but I expect you knew a way, didn't you? Let's get in the car now and wrap a couple of blankets round you to warm you up a bit. Dr Harraday's here too.' She felt the slight jump in Charly's bones, and went on quickly, 'Oh, come on, you know him, he's nice! Anyway he's going to do the driving, which he's very good at, as a matter of fact!'

Half an hour later they were well on the road back to London. Simon had stopped to telephone, leaving Vicky to hold Charly in the back of the car in her cocoon of blankets. She didn't need to be told to watch her, just in case the disturbed girl suddenly tried to leap out of the car and run away, though Charly seemed far too exhausted to do that. She fell into a deep sleep as soon as Simon came back to the car again and didn't wake when he stopped unexpectedly a little later on and turned round to Vicky with a brief, 'I've got another phone call I want to make.'

It seemed to take him quite a little while, but suddenly he was there, opening the car door quietly, his face carved into odd shadows by the bright lights on the road behind him. He glanced at the two in the back, hesitated, and then said quietly,

'You can come in the front now. I don't think she'll wake, and David's got child-locks on those doors.'

Charly had curled into a corner, pulling away from Vicky in sleep, so there didn't seem any harm in his suggestion. Vicky climbed stiffly into the front. Perhaps Simon wanted to give her his next instructions, tell her what he was going to do with Charly now. Looking at him as he drove on, at the strong hands on the wheel, the aloof, aristocratic profile, Vicky felt a throb of sudden total love for the man who had treated her so abominably all day. But he had spent a whole day out of his busy life, hunting for a lost child. All she wanted to do at the moment was look at him with the warmth of love sweeping through her, and a tingling knowledge that in spite of his moods, his coldness, his temper, he could light in her a response which no one else could ever match.

He seemed to be able to feel her gaze—because he spoke abruptly, though softly because of the sleeping child in the back. 'What was it—just a feeling?'

'What? Oh, stubbornness really, I think. I just thought she had to be here.'

'You were right about the dark. I think she'd have stayed in hiding without that.' He paused briefly, then, 'You know I'll have to take her home, don't you? I can't admit her to the clinic when she's not officially my patient, and besides, we're not equipped to deal with her.' As if he could feel Vicky's instinctive protest he added, 'But I have just been in touch with a private psychiatric place which could take her if Ryder agrees. I got the superintendent on the phone just now.'

He was right, of course. The clinic wasn't equipped to deal with a disturbed anorexic who needed psychiatric care. Vicky's protest stilled. She took a quick glance round at Charly in the back, but the girl was still asleep. After several moments, when Simon didn't say any more, she found herself tugged again by the love and longing she felt for the man by her side. His face, she thought, still had its grim lines in the lights which lit him dimly.

'Can we talk about something else?' she asked hesitantly.

'If you want to.'

The tone wasn't promising. It almost sounded as if he meant, *if you must*. Vicky said very quickly,

'You misunderstood something this morning. I don't have any feelings for Andrew at all any more—in—in fact I think I probably always *did* think of him as a brother, really! Never having had one, I . . .'

She left it there, hoping Simon would answer. He didn't. Vicky glanced at him almost in exasperation. 'I thought when the bell went that it was *you* who'd forgotten your key! Anyway I—I was actually quite decent! And if you made anything out of seeing me patting Andrew's arm, I was merely trying, rather impatiently, to get him to realise that he had to see Marina's point of view sometimes if he wanted to make his marriage work!' She swallowed hard, knowing that there was a touch of despair in having to mention Marina, and finished, 'That was all!'

There was silence for a moment, long enough for her to wonder if Simon was going to say anything at all. Then the deep voice came, with less of the coldness in it than before. 'Ah. I see. Well, just now, after I'd rung the psychiatrist, I put a call through to Marina. At least to the place where I guessed she'd be. She was, too. She'd run back to Dick—the man she was living with before she married her farmer. She wasn't getting much change out of Dick, I'm glad to say,' he added drily. 'I gather he's spent the last twenty-four hours telling her to pull herself together!'

'I thought she was living with *you*!'

'Good God no. That wouldn't have lasted five minutes! She was living with one of my closest friends. They'd been together for about two years,' Simon said casually. There was a pause while Vicky digested this information and then he said, very thoughtfully, '*That* was what you meant about . . . Come to think of it, there've been quite a few remarks of that sort, haven't there? About not wanting to be a stand-in, for instance?'

'You certainly gave me the impression—' Vicky swallowed. She could feel a flush rising into her cheeks. She could also feel joy spreading through her, and a desire to break into laughter about the whole situation. Simon said calmly,

'Just to update you on Marina, I told her in no uncertain terms to go back to her husband and stop bothering everybody. I also told her that he'd come looking for her, and you may be glad to know that *that* made her burst into tears and say she was going home at once. She's probably on her way right now.' His voice took on its velvety note. 'You really are an emotional family. Screaming tempers and floods of tears at every turn. I wonder what I'm getting into? But you must have misunderstood me about the bride, because the one I really fancied was the bridesmaid.'

There was a sudden whimper from the back. Vicky turned round swiftly, to see Charly stirring, and at once she was all nurse, all soothing, quiet words, making sure the child knew she was still there. She had to go on keeping an eye on Charly, too, as the young girl went on

moving fitfully in and out of sleep. She didn't settle again
until they were right into London. All the time, just the
same, Vicky was aware of Simon driving on quietly,
leaving her to it, trusting her to handle it. And all the
time a corner of her mind was aware that he had just
said . . .

When at last she managed to turn back to the front
again she looked quickly at Simon, but he said only,

'Has she settled right down again? Good—in that case
I'll drop you off at home and take her on alone. It isn't
far. And you'd only have a lot of hanging about to do,
otherwise.'

'Shouldn't I—?'

'No. Better to play things down, on ethical grounds.
We shouldn't encourage dependency, either, when
she'll be going somewhere else.'

He swung the car into suddenly familiar streets before
she could argue any further and not more than moments
later he was drawing up very gently at the entrance to
Belville Close. 'I'll put you down here to save turning.
Oh, and Vicky?'

'Yes?' She turned back to the window, which he had
wound down as she got out of the car with quiet care.

'I'll be back as soon as I can.' There was a glint in the
dark eyes looking up at her. 'Don't go out.'

She stared after the car as he accelerated carefully
away, her heart suddenly beating in an uneven bump.

She let herself into the house, trying not to tremble
with anticipation. They must have left the lights on this
morning, she thought absently—they'd gone out in such
a hurry. She ran lightly up the stairs, crossed the sitting-
room and paused to gaze into the kitchen with a sudden
longing for a cup of tea. No, she'd have a bath first, just
to get the chill out of her bones, and change into
something she looked really nice in and brush her hair
out loose, and then . . . She could hear music coming
from somewhere—next door must be being a lot noisier

than usual. She found herself doing a little dance step to the beat, bumped into a table, and stifled a laugh. She was feeling as crazy as if she'd been given the world for a present. Well, perhaps she had. Perhaps—

A door opened somewhere and a girl's voice, from the floor above, called down,

'Hey, Si, is that you? The job folded on me, so I'm back home earlier than we expected. All in one piece, you'll be glad to hear.'

A pair of long and beautiful legs in tight jeans appeared on the stairs with the last words and turned into a tall and beautiful girl with dark hair and a strikingly pretty face. Her fine eyebrows went up at the sight of Vicky, and she said with surprise,

'Oh, hi! I thought it was Si coming in—is he with you?'

'No.'

'I'm Caroline. I live here with Si. Well, I do most of the time, but I've been away on a modelling job in the States. Should have gone on for another six weeks, too. Sad, that.' She gave Vicky a grin, with a touch of curiosity in it—perhaps for the way Vicky was staring at her wordlessly. 'Did Si let you in and go away again, or—oh, I see! Is it your stuff in the other room upstairs?'

'Yes. Yes, it is. I'm—'

'Oho!' Caroline said thoughtfully. She seemed to be regarding Vicky with amusement rather than anger. 'I know who you are, then. Sorry, but I looked because I couldn't think who'd be in there. Your name's Vicky Jardine, isn't it? Hallo, then, Vicky.' She smiled again with apparent good humour. 'Si's imported you in my absence. Well, well.' She drew out the words on a mischievous note. 'Sorry if I stunned you with my presence—have you just come off duty? And are you working for him as well as living here? Oh, d'you want a cup of coffee, by the way? I think I'll make one.'

Vicky was feeling totally numb. 'No thanks,' she managed, as Caroline turned away towards the kitchen.

She was struggling against disbelief, shock, and a sense of utter blankness. 'I—I think I'll just go up and . . .'

'The shower's on the blink again,' Caroline imparted over her shoulder. 'Maybe it's something I do to it, I don't know, Si's always getting mad with me about it.' She turned her head to give Vicky another interested look and her mouth curved again in a sudden amused, mocking grin. 'You're ever so quiet, Vicky—am I overwhelming you?'

Vicky found herself moving. She was up the stairs to her bedroom on swift feet. She didn't know if she'd made any kind of polite answer to Caroline, or not. She pulled her bedroom door shut behind her and leaned against it on suddenly weak legs. Caroline. *Caroline* lived here. Caroline whose name had never been mentioned by Simon. Caroline who wasn't expected back yet!

She couldn't just stand here with her numbness turning into a tight knot of misery in her stomach. She walked across and sat down on the edge of her bed. What had she just been going to do—have a bath? She pulled the pins out of her hair absently and shook her head to let it fall loosely down, before she realised that she couldn't just go on doing whatever it was she had been going to do, just as if her whole life hadn't suddenly cracked apart.

Surely Simon couldn't be that dishonest . . . ?

Perhaps it didn't seem like that to him. Caroline was away. Vicky was here.

She heard Caroline come up the stairs and go into the room opposite, whistling cheerfully. It was a tune Simon often whistled in the shower. Somehow the sound woke Vicky out of her trance into real pain. Suddenly she was scrambling out of her uniform and into the first other clothes which came to hand—her dungarees with a jumper pulled over the top—and she was reaching under the bed for her suitcase. *Don't go out*, Simon had said, without knowing that he was going to come home to find Caroline was back. Well, she *was* going out. She was going home! She was sick of London with its casual relationships. She couldn't take any more. She couldn't take hurting all over and feeling foolish and knowing that she'd been out of her depth all along without realising it.

She thrust on a jacket and came cautiously out of her room with her roughly-packed suitcase in her hand. She didn't even know what she'd put into it but there'd be other old things at home. She blinked fiercely, swallowing the lump in her throat. Soft music came from behind the closed door opposite and she could hear Caroline humming to it and moving around opening and shutting drawers. Vicky stole down the stairs, feeling stupid for wanting to leave surreptitiously, knowing it showed her lack of sophistication, but feeling a growing glow of anger—at herself, at Simon. She couldn't even bear to think about Simon. There'd be time enough to grieve over him later, she supposed desolately. At least she could leave without seeing him, without embarrassing him—if he was capable of being embarrassed. She had reached street level, and was beginning to put out her hand to the front door, when it opened.

Simon came through it with his dark hair looking blown, and his eyes narrowing against the light. He stopped dead, just as Vicky stopped dead. His eyebrows went up. There was a moment's absolute silence as he took in her coat, her suitcase, the wide eyes which had flown to his face. He said, on a note which sounded like concern,

'Vicky—?'

'Your girlfriend's back. She's upstairs.' She blurted the words, and they came out sounding fierce. She was glad about that, it was better than sounding heart-broken. She reached for dignity as she added, 'I'm just going.'

He slammed the front door shut and set his back against it. There was a look in his eyes which was half-mystified, half-angry. '*Who* did you say was upstairs?' he demanded.

'Your girlfriend. Caroline!' As she saw comprehension come into his eyes, and even *amusement*, her anger flashed into a satisfying sarcasm. 'Had you forgotten Caroline?' she enquired. 'I didn't gather she'd been away *that* long—'

'Ah. *That* Caroline. And where did you say you were going?' he asked silkily, the deep voice at its most velvet.

'Oh, home for the weekend! I just felt like it! I haven't been up for ages and I'm sure you two would like to be alone!'

'It isn't the weekend,' Simon pointed out on the same silky note. His shoulders came away from the door. He took a step forward with such obvious menace that Vicky flinched. 'I haven't given you time off, either, as far as I remember. So you can't go anywhere!'

'I *can*!'

Her suitcase was suddenly seized out of her hand and dumped on the floor. Her jacket was whipped away from her shoulders and thrown down after it. 'No, you can't,' Simon said forcefully, 'you're coming upstairs to say hallo to Caroline nicely. Oh yes you are, Vicky. *Up*, I said. You either go on your own two feet or I'll pick you up in a fireman's lift and carry you!'

He meant it. And there was an awful lot of him, strong and well-muscled, let alone the alarming jut of his jaw which showed exactly how determined he was to get his own way. Vicky turned and stalked up the stairs ahead of him with angry dignity and with her heart turning unhappy cartwheels in and out of her stomach. How *could* he? And how could she still feel torn with love for him?

Simon kept a tight grip on her arm, which he had seized to show that he really would lift her off her feet if she didn't obey him. He marched her into the sitting room, looked round, glanced upwards as an odd banging noise came from above. Vicky kept her shoulder deliberately turned on him in spite of his grip on her upper arm, and found herself thrust further across the room.

'Hey! Stop your bloody aerobic dancing, and come down here!' Simon bellowed.

It seemed Caroline was used to being yelled at like that, because the banging stopped and her voice floated down cheerfully, if distantly. 'Okay, I hear you, what have I done now?' A door opened above, and the voice came more clearly. 'You might at least sound a bit more welcoming!'

As she appeared on the stairs Simon moved behind Vicky, imprisoning both her arms and pulling her back against him. Above her head he said, 'I want you to meet Vicky, that's all. Vicky, this is my sister Cat.'

'We've met,' Caroline said, at the same time as Vicky, trying to twist round to look at him, brought out,

'Cat isn't short for Caroline!'

'In our family it is. There are,' Simon said, continuing to restrain her, but leaning forward enough for her to catch the gleam of amusement in his eyes, 'too many of us to bother with full names. I told you, four sisters—Mel, Steph, Cat and Liz. And this one, for my sins, is Cat!'

'Oh,' Caroline said, on a long note. Her eyes were round with startled alarm. 'Oh lord! I'm *sorry*. Didn't I say he was my brother? Did you think—'

'Your nuisance value is even higher than usual,' her brother said smoothly. Vicky said nothing at all. She was feeling too foolish and too glad. She could feel the length of Simon's body hard and warm against her, sending a tingle up her spine, but the see-saw of emotions she had just gone through seemed to have paralysed her. She could see, suddenly, that Caroline was like Simon—the height scaled down into femininity, the dark hair, even the same aristocratic nose. It just hadn't occurred to her, she thought weakly. She felt a slight tremor run through Simon, and she thought he might be laughing, but his voice was quite solemn and even a little caustic as he went on speaking to his sister.

'You can make up for it right now, by going out. Yes, I know you've only just come home, but I'm sure you've got lots of friends you can go and see!'

'Yes, okay, I will in a minute.' Caroline was giving Vicky a ruefully amused look now and she flashed her a grin. 'He's an awful bully, had you noticed? But I really am sorry if—'

'*Out*, Cat! Now! I really don't intend trying to persuade this girl to marry me right in front of you!'

'Oh, if it's like *that*!' Caroline grinned broadly again, but began to move hastily. 'If somebody's got you that far,' she said in flight, 'don't for goodness' sake let me stop you. We've been trying to get rid of you for years—I just wish you luck, Vicky, that's all, because he really is appallingly bossy! Hey, can I just go back and get my coat? Oh no, I left it downstairs in the dining-room. I'm going round to Yvonne's, if anyone wants me!'

A chuckle floated back up the stairs. A moment later the front door banged and Simon turned Vicky round to face him.

She looked up, sheepishly. There was a quizzical expression in his dark eyes and his mouth held a faintly sardonic curve. His arms held her lightly, but one hand moved up into the curls at the back of her neck. Vicky had the sudden feeling that if he was going to go on looking at her like that, she was going to stop breathing. He said, very softly, 'What *you* need is a ball and chain. But let's get one thing clear. *Do* you not love me, or *will* you not?'

'Oh, I do!'

'Good. Because I'm quite dotty about *you*.' His lips came down to touch her forehead in the lightest of caresses. 'If you'll just hold still long enough for me to get near you, I might be able to tell you so. I've some-times wondered if I'm going to end up marrying you or murdering you!'

'Either will do,' Vicky said dizzily. She wasn't even sure what she was saying, because the sheer magnetism of him was sending shivers of delight all over her and she slid her hands round inside his jacket to hold on to him in case she fell apart. Her cheek went against his heart to hear its thump rise in tempo, matching her own.

'Oh, I think the love-and-marriage bit would be bet-ter, don't you?' His voice sounded like a soft burr through his chest and a hand slid down her back to pull her even closer against him. 'Yes? Hey, stop hiding down there when I want to kiss you!'

She raised her face obediently, her eyes starry. The dark gaze of his seemed to mesmerise her, but he pulled back, and there was a sudden grin edging his mouth. 'No, over *there*,' he commanded suddenly, moving both of them towards the sofa. 'Let's go back to where we were so rudely interrupted.'

He dumped her unceremoniously down on the cushions, letting go of her so abruptly that she fell in an undignified heap. Then he strode across the room and took the phone off the hook. 'We've done enough today, and David's on call. I'm not going to tell you all about *anything* just now, so don't ask. Talking can wait.'

The tall form came back across the room towards her. Vicky watched him with her heart in her eyes and a deep tremor of longing inside her for the hardness of his arms around her again. He caught her to him with a sharply indrawn breath, his eyes beginning to glow with a deep light, his mouth curving in pure pleasure. Close against her he murmured,

'Now, angel, I'm tired of being driven crazy, so where *were* we with that unfinished business . . . ?'

4 Doctor Nurse Romances
FREE

Coping with the daily tragedies and ordeals of a busy hospital, and sharing the satisfaction of a difficult job well done, people find themselves unexpectedly drawn together. Mills & Boon Doctor Nurse Romances capture perfectly the excitement, the intrigue and the emotions of modern medicine, that so often lead to overwhelming and blissful love. By becoming a regular reader of Mills & Boon Doctor Nurse Romances you can enjoy EIGHT superb new titles every two months plus a whole range of special benefits: your very own personal membership card, a free newsletter packed with recipes, competitions, bargain book offers, plus big cash savings.

**AND an Introductory FREE GIFT for YOU.
Turn over the page for details.**